PUFFIN

THE RAG AND BONE SHOP

Robert Cormier was born in 1925 and lived in Leominster in
M... ...achusetts, USA. He began writing at school where he
...aised for his poetry. At the age of nineteen he had his
...ort story published when a college teacher, Florence
..., sent one of his stories to a national magazine without
...owledge. He began his professional writing career
...ng radio commercials and went on to become an
... winning journalist.

...Cormier became a full-time writer after the successful
...ion of his first novel for teenagers, *The Chocolate War*
...ed in the UK in 1975), followed by others such as *I*
...Cheese and *After the First Death*. He was concerned
...ne problems facing young people in modern society
... concern was reflected in his novels. He soon
...ed a reputation as a brilliant and uncompromising

...le, caring, family-orientated man, Robert Cormier was
...d with three daughters, a son and many grandchildren.
He ...d in November 2000.

Praise for Robert Cormier

The Chocolate War
...his is a *tour de force*, and a *tour de force* of
realism' – *Times Educational Supplement*

The Bumblebee Flies Anyway
'A novel you are unlikely to forget'
– *Times Educational Supplement*

Other books by Robert Cormier

CORMIER

The Rag and Bone Shop

PUFFIN BOOKS

PUFFIN BOOKS

Published by the Penguin Group
Penguin Books Ltd, 80 Strand, London WC2R 0RL, England
Penguin Putnam Inc., 375 Hudson Street, New York, New York 10014, USA
Penguin Books Australia Ltd, 250 Camberwell Road, Camberwell, Victoria 3124, Australia
Penguin Books Canada Ltd, 10 Alcorn Avenue, Toronto, Ontario, Canada M4V 3B2
Penguin Books India (P) Ltd, 11 Community Centre, Panchsheel Park, New Delhi – 110 017, India
Penguin Books (NZ) Ltd, Cnr Rosedale and Airborne Roads, Albany, Auckland, New Zealand
Penguin Books (South Africa) (Pty) Ltd, 24 Sturdee Avenue, Rosebank 2196, South Africa

Penguin Books Ltd, Registered Offices: 80 Strand, London WC2R 0RL, England

www.penguin.com

First published in the USA by Delacorte Press, an imprint of Random House Children's
Books, 2001
Published in Great Britain by Hamish Hamilton Ltd 2001
Published in Puffin Books 2002

Copyright © Robert Cormier, 2001
All rights reserved

Made and printed in England by Clays Ltd, St Ives plc

British Library Cataloguing in Publication Data
A CIP catalogue record for this book is available from the British Library

ISBN 0–141–31444–3

PART I

"Feeling better?"

"I guess so. My headache's gone. Is there a connection?"

"Maybe. They say confession's good for the soul. But I don't know if it eliminates headaches."

"Am I supposed to say I'm sorry now?"

"The fact that you confessed indicates a degree of sorrow."

"Is that enough?"

"That's up to you, Carl. What you did can't be erased, of course."

"I know. They're dead. Gone. Can't bring them back. But—can the sin be erased?"

"I can't tell you that. I'm not a priest."

"But I confessed to you."

"Yes, but I can't give you absolution."

Pause.

"Are the police coming?"

"They're waiting outside."

Trent shut off the tape player and leaned back in the chair, kneaded the flesh above his eyebrows. In the silence of the office, he still heard Carl Seaton's voice, all cunning gone, penitent, full of regret. Trent had sat across from him for four hours, under the harsh light of a 100-watt ceiling bulb, in the small cluttered office. The relentless questions and answers, the evasions and rationalizations, the eventual admission (not the same as a confession), and, finally, the confession itself.

The Trent magic touch at work, as a newspaper headline had once proclaimed. But Trent felt no particular magic now, no thrill of accomplishment. Too many confessions? Like Carl Seaton's? Having induced Carl to confess (that old Trent magic has you in its spell), Trent had had to listen to the recitation of his cold-blooded, deliberate murder of three people. The victims were a thirty-five-year-old woman, her thirty-seven-year-old husband and their ten-year-old son, although Carl hadn't known their ages at the time.

Six months ago, in the milky whiteness of a winter dawn, Carl Seaton had broken into the modest two-story home of Aaron and Muriel Stone to steal the small gun collection in the cellar. He admitted that he knew nothing about guns except the pleasure of holding them in his hands and the sense of power they gave him. Carl Seaton broke a cellar window, not worried about the noise of his intrusion, having learned that the family was away on vacation and that there was no alarm system.

He was disappointed to find that there were only three small guns in the so-called collection. He was surprised to find that the guns were loaded. He then decided to search the house. Thought he might find something of value, although he knew nothing about fencing stolen goods. Heard a noise from the second floor. Padded toward the stairs, his sneakers noiseless in the carpeted hallway. Upstairs, he entered a bedroom and was surprised to see a man and woman asleep in the bed. The woman slightly curled up, the bedclothes thrown off. Beautiful eyelashes, thick and curved. The husband flat on his back, mouth open, snoring gently. Carl became conscious of the gun in his hand, felt suddenly the power of his position. What it must feel like to be— God. Looking down at them, so helpless and defenseless, it occurred to him that he could do anything he wanted with them. They were at his mercy. He wondered what the woman would look like without her blue nightgown on. He had never seen an actual naked woman, only in magazines, movies and videos. But it was too much of a bother now to think about that. He didn't want to spoil this nice feeling, just standing there, knowing he was in charge. He raised the gun and shot them. First, the man. The bullet exploded through the thin blanket, small shreds of green cloth filling the air like rain, the noise of the shot not as loud as he'd imagined it would be. As the woman leaped awake, her eyes flying open, he shot her in the mouth, marveled at the gush of blood and the way her eyes became fixed and frozen in shock. A mighty sneeze shook his body, the smell of gunpowder heavy in the air.

He wondered: Was there anybody else in the house who might have heard the shots? He went

6

into the hallway, opened a door at the far end, saw a boy sleeping in a bed shaped almost like a boat, hair in neat bangs on his forehead. The boy's eyelids fluttered. Carl wondered whether he should shoot him or not. Then decided that the boy would be better off if he did. Terrible thing to wake up and find your mother and father dead. Murdered. Carl shot the boy as an act of kindness, nodding, feeling good about it, generous.

Carl Seaton had confessed his acts of murder almost eagerly, glad to provide the details that would lead to his own doom, his voice buoyant with relief. Which was often the case with those who finally acknowledged their acts.

Trent felt only contempt for Carl Seaton, although he had simulated sympathy and compassion during the interrogation. Acting was only another facet of interrogating subjects. If he felt any compassion at the moment, it was for Carl Seaton's parents. Carl was seventeen years old.

Trent's jaw began to ache. He never got headaches, instead this streak of pain running along his jaw. Ridiculous, but there it was. It usually happened after an interrogation, like a punishment he had to endure. Why a punishment? *I'm only doing my job.* That's the trouble, Lottie had claimed.

And now he admitted why Carl Seaton's confession, another notch in his belt, had failed to provide the usual surge of triumph. There was no Lottie in his life now to tell about it, even though he knew she had stopped listening at the end. Still, Lottie had always been there for him, even if he hadn't always been there for her.

The pain in his jaw increased and he tried yawning to provide some relief. He resisted taking the painkillers in his desk drawer. Maybe I deserve some pain, he thought, thinking of Lottie.

He put away the cassette and tape player, cleaned up his desk, checked tomorrow's appointments. Time to go home. Home to the empty house, where Lottie was only a forlorn ghost. But there was no place else to go.

PART II

Classes in Monument ended on the last Friday of June for the summer vacation but Jason Dorrant regarded today, Monday, as the first real day of vacation. The weekend just past didn't count because he never went to school on weekends anyway.

He had intended to sleep late this morning but his eyes flew open as if the alarm clock had rung. The digital clock said 6:32 and Jason smiled, stretching luxuriously, thinking of the lazy summer days that lay ahead. Not exactly lazy—summer day camp started next week—but no more classes and no more homework for the next two months.

Actually, he'd had a pretty good year at

Monument Middle School. He'd managed, for the very first time, to sneak onto the honor roll for the second marking period, although he figured that was due to luck rather than brainpower. He was glad that the seventh grade was behind him and he hoped eighth grade would be easier. He had a feeling that it wouldn't be, though. He always had to work hard for his grades. Other kids seemed to fly through the terms with good marks on tests, answering questions in class, their hands waving eagerly at the teacher, but Jason was shy about offering answers even when he knew them. He didn't like to be the center of attention. He'd feel the heat of his blood beating in his cheeks and his heart racing dangerously.

Anyway, school was not on his schedule for the next two months. He sighed, stretched his legs again and threw off the thin blanket. He knew that summer camp would be no picnic, either, but at least there wouldn't be any classrooms or written tests and he could make a fresh start with new kids. Leave the old kids behind, especially those who made his life miserable. Not that they were cruel or mean or made him the object of pranks or tortured him or anything like that. Mostly, they ignored him. He was rarely asked to join in their games or activities. He usually sat alone in the cafeteria and *felt* alone even when others were at the table. The other students seldom talked to him or asked him his opinion about anything. When they did encounter him in situations where he couldn't be avoided, they addressed him in an absentminded way, didn't seem interested in what he had to say, quickly turned their attention elsewhere.

He liked the company of younger kids. They paid attention to him, listened to him, laughed at his jokes. He got along great with his sister, Emma, who was eight and liked to follow him around. At recess, he'd sometimes wander over to the other side of the schoolyard and watch the second and third graders playing their games. He got a kick out of them, the way they acted so serious, like miniature grown-ups. He'd push them on their swings. He'd seek out Emma, who was always glad to see him. He knew that Emma was smarter than he was. She read two or three books a week, while Jason had to struggle to get through a book, like Stephen King's new one, even though he was enjoying it. Emma was a great writer, too. She'd won an essay contest last year. The essay, which she titled "Rites and Wrongs," was about the celebrations of holidays and how they had changed through the years. She explained the title to him, how *rites* was a play on the word *rights,* what she called a pun. What he liked about Emma was that she didn't explain things in a way that made him feel stupid but as if she was sharing knowledge with him and making him feel worthy of that sharing.

He got out of bed, heard the sound of the shower from the bathroom next to his bedroom. His mother was an early riser and could not function in the morning until, one, she drank a cup of black coffee, and, two, she had a shower. Emma, too, was an early riser but she would read in bed for an hour or two. His dad was away on a business trip to Lincoln, Nebraska. He would be home in three days. His father was a fanatic about football, had a season ticket to the New England Patriots games. Jason went with him sometimes but could not get excited about twenty-two men knocking each other around on a football field. He liked to be with his father, though, and pretended that he liked the game. He always had to act real sad and upset when the Patriots lost. His father went into what his mother called a blue funk when the Patriots were defeated.

Sitting on the edge of the bed, Jason contemplated the day that lay ahead. He would accompany his mother to the Y as her guest in the morning and do some swimming in the free swim period while she went through her exercises on the machines. Home for lunch and he'd be free for the afternoon while his mother did her volunteer work at Monument Hospital. Emma would be spending the day at Kim Cambridge's house. Kim's family had a swimming pool. Emma had invited Jason to tag along but he was looking forward to a free afternoon when he could do anything he pleased. Goof around, maybe take a bike ride, watch television or finish the Stephen King book. Brad Bartlett had invited him for a dip into *his* swimming pool in the afternoon but Jason knew that he had been invited simply because their mothers served on a lot of committees together. Brad liked to play practical jokes and you could never trust what he was going to do. Jason liked his kid sister, Alicia. She was a whiz at jigsaw puzzles and he liked to watch the picture emerge as she set the pieces in place. So maybe he might drop in to see her later today, but wouldn't bring his swimming trunks.

Anyway, the day loomed ahead, free, no classes, no demands, not even any household chores that he knew about, and he lay there feasting on the thought of the long summer days ahead.

The body of seven-year-old Alicia Bartlett was found between the trunks of two overlapping maple trees in dense woods only five hundred yards from her home. She was covered with an accumulation of leaves, branches and debris, which was one of the reasons her body had not been discovered during the first search of the area.

Whoever killed her had apparently laid her down with tenderness, folded her arms across her chest, pulled her dress down primly to her knees and carefully arranged her long black hair to frame her face. But the killer could not erase the expression frozen in her eyes—horror and surprise—and had not bothered to close those stricken eyes.

Her body was discovered at dusk during the second search of the area by a volunteer who spotted a small white sandal sticking out of a pile of debris. Authorities reasoned that an animal had perhaps disturbed her covering, exposing the sandal sometime between the first and second searches.

The medical examiner listed the preliminary cause of death as head trauma from an irregularly shaped blunt instrument. Alicia had been struck in the temple with a single blow and death was probably instantaneous. The weapon was not found. She had not been raped or sexually molested. There was a minimum of blood in the area of the wound. The child had not resisted her attacker, since there was no defensive evidence such as blood or bits of flesh under the fingernails. Time of death was placed at approximately 5 P.M., less than an hour after her disappearance.

Alicia had last been seen on the patio of her home by twelve-year-old Jason Dorrant, who lived in her neighborhood, about four o'clock on the afternoon of June twenty-ninth. She had either wandered off or been lured away a few minutes before her mother arrived home from a shopping trip at 4:10 P.M.

Alicia Bartlett was small for her age, fragile, intelligent, friendly and outgoing, although her mother said she was timid with strangers and certainly would not have gone off with someone she did not know. She was an utterly feminine child, which was the reason she was wearing a dress on one of the hottest days of early summer, refusing to put on the shorts and brief halter her mother had suggested. The dress, a green sleeveless one, was probably just as cool as any other outfit, her mother had decided.

Alicia lived with her parents, Norman and Laura Bartlett, and her thirteen-year-old brother, Brad, in a section of Monument, Massachusetts, known as Cobb's Creek, named for the brook that meandered along the edges of the neighborhood. Searchers had at first concentrated on the brook, even though its depth was seldom more than a foot in most places and it would be dried up in spots by midsummer. Still, it was feared that Alicia might have stumbled and fallen into the stream, struck her head on a rock, lost consciousness and drowned. The focus on the brook was another reason that her body had been overlooked in the early stages of the search.

Detective Lieutenant George Braxton was in charge of the investigation. On the evening of that first day, Senator Harold Gibbons arrived at police headquarters. Although Braxton greeted him cordially—the senator's grandson had been a classmate of the seven-year-old victim—he felt that the senator was an unnecessary distraction and an annoyance.

Braxton had a lot of things to be annoyed about. At forty-seven years of age, he was an insomniac with an inability to relax, whether in bed or in his office. He both loved and hated his job. He loved it because he had a sense of doing good, using his wits to put lawbreakers in jail, although he never put those feelings into words, knowing how corny they sounded. He hated it because of cases like this one—no clues, no leads, no physical evidence. The presence of the media and the intrusion of Senator Gibbons cast a further spotlight on a case that was already too public, too open to scrutiny. The final irritation was the presence of District Attorney Alvin Dark, who had taken up residence in Braxton's office and, Braxton knew, was waiting to take over the investigation if something definite wasn't done in the next twenty-four hours.

Braxton spent the night in his office, getting nowhere. As dawn arrived, the detective lifted a slat of the venetian blind, opened the window and stared dismally at the bleak, sunless streets, the oppressive clouds hovering over the downtown buildings. He could feel, even at this early hour, heat rising from the pavement, like an invisible soot he could almost taste. He had not slept for twenty-four hours.

He had no clues, no leads, no evidence.

He did have a possible suspect, depending on the result of an interview he planned to conduct later this morning.

J ason Dorrant found it hard to believe that Alicia Bartlett was dead. Not only dead but murdered. Attacked and hit hard enough to kill her. He could not imagine anyone bad enough, evil enough, to do something like that. Especially to a nice little kid like Alicia. With her little-old-lady features, her big teeth too large for her mouth and the sprinkle of freckles, which she hated, on her cheeks.

He felt his chin wobbling a bit and his eyes beginning to fill with tears. He didn't want to cry. A long time ago, he had made a promise not to cry anymore. He used to cry a lot when he was just a little kid, like if he heard a noise at night and thought a burglar was breaking in. But that was kid stuff and didn't count. The crying that really counted happened later at school, when he worried about not having finished his homework or when he didn't know the answer to a question the teacher asked or even when he *did* know the answer but was afraid, too scared to raise his hand. Let's get this straight: he didn't really cry but his chin would begin to wobble all over the place and tears would fill his eyes and he'd have to hold himself rigid to make it all stop. But he couldn't always make it stop.

Then the fight with Bobo Kelton happened and changed everything. That was when he vowed not to cry any more. Not during the fight but afterward. And it wasn't even a fight but one sweet and beautiful blow that sent Bobo to the floor. The surprise and the shock on Bobo's face had been terrific to see.

Here's how it happened: Bobo pushed him from behind while they were waiting in line in the school cafeteria. But that wasn't the real reason Jason had turned around and knocked him down. The real reason was all the things that Jason had seen Bobo do over the course of the year. Sly stuff. Tripping someone, pulling a guy's shirt out of his pants, slamming a locker door so that Johnny Moran's fingers got caught and jammed. Nobody did anything about Bobo. Merely accepted his actions. Or maybe didn't see his mean little tricks. But Jason prided himself on his powers of observation. When you're an outsider, and not part of the bunch, you're in a position to see what others don't see. And Jason was a witness to Bobo's worst act of all. What he did to Rebecca Tolland.

The day before the incident in the cafeteria Jason had seen Bobo Kelton, during the change of classes, walk right up to Rebecca Tolland, who had stopped by her locker. He pushed his body against hers. He whispered something in her ear and Rebecca shook her head in shock and anger. Bobo drew away, then reached out and actually pinched her chest. Tweaked one of her small breasts. It all happened in a few seconds as students rushed by, too intent on hurrying to the next class to notice what was going on. Jason watched as Bobo walked away, leaving Rebecca standing there, pale and trembling. Hearing the warning bell, Jason went off, heart pounding with fury, knowing that Bobo would probably get away with what he'd done. Jason doubted that Rebecca would report the incident and he was right.

The next day, Bobo pushed Jason lightly from behind as they stood in line in the cafeteria. Whirling around, Jason pushed Bobo back, shoving both hands against his chest. Bobo stepped back, surprise on his face. Remembering what Bobo had done to Rebecca and all his other mean stuff, Jason hit Bobo with his clenched fist, astonishing himself as well as Bobo. Blood spurted from Bobo's nostrils as he fell backward, landing on his butt with a howl of pain.

Looking up at Jason as he wiped the blood from his face, he cried out: "What did you do that for?" Like a little boy, his own chin wobbling. Jason was swept with a thrilling sense of triumph and stood there grinning. Bobo was taken to the dispensary and Jason was ushered to the principal's office and made to sit alone for the next two periods. Finally, Mr. Hobart, the principal, called him into his office and made a speech. About violence and how it did not solve problems. And how unprovoked violence was the worst kind of all. Unprovoked? Jason knew immediately what the word meant, although he had never heard it before. "A slight push which may have been accidental from a fellow classmate does not warrant that kind of retaliation," Mr. Hobart said. Jason knew he could not tell him what he had seen Bobo do to Rebecca Tolland because that would only embarrass Rebecca. Jason listened to Mr. Hobart going on about violence and the uselessness of revenge and he nodded, but all the time, he was happy. He had done something. He had taken action. He had socked Bobo Kelton. Given him a bloody nose. He didn't think he'd ever hit anybody again but he had proved himself capable of doing it. And at that same moment, in Mr. Hobart's office, letting the principal's words fill the air but not his ears, he vowed never to cry again. He wasn't sure of the connection between hitting Bobo Kelton and not crying anymore but it was there, all right.

The incident did not change his life. Rebecca Tolland did not rush into his arms like she'd have done if this had been a movie. In fact, she ignored him, as usual. He was still timid and hated to answer questions in class. His classmates looked at him curiously for a day or two but nobody passed any remarks, didn't cheer for him but didn't boo him, either. Bobo steered clear of him. Jason still ate alone, mostly, in the cafeteria or silently when at a table with other guys. Sometimes Danny Edison, another outsider, sat next to him but they didn't say much of anything to each other.

But Jason had not cried since that day. No tears on his cheeks or quivering chin. Until now, in his room, thinking of what happened to Alicia Bartlett and his chin wobbling all over the place.

He turned away as Emma entered the room, not knocking as usual, which sometimes irritated him, but he was glad for her appearance now. He composed himself, got his chin under control as he heard her say: "Too bad about Alicia Bartlett." Pause, then: "You okay, Jason?"

He nodded, looking out the window.

"You liked her a lot, didn't you?"

Jason nodded again, watching a police cruiser driving slowly along the street. He craned his neck, watching its progress.

"Didn't you always help her with her jigsaw puzzles?" Emma asked.

Jason watched the cruiser make a U-turn three houses away.

"I didn't really help her. She was real good with the puzzles. But I got a kick out of her."

"I didn't really like her," Emma said.

Jason turned to her in surprise because Alicia had always reminded him of Emma.

"Oh, I know you're supposed to say good things about someone who dies. But I thought she was a pain in the neck. Always acted like she was better than anyone else. Always wore those dresses. And she was only seven years old, for criminy's sake."

Jason looked at Emma as if he had never seen her before. But maybe she was right. Alicia got on his nerves sometimes. She could be moody, didn't feel like talking on certain days, and sent him home once, saying she wasn't in the mood for company. But most of the time he was amused by her little-old-lady ways and she listened to what he had to say, which was more than he could say for a lot of other people.

"But I'm sorry she had to die. In that horrible way," Emma said.

"I'm sorry, too," Jason said.

"Do you think I'm horrible? For saying what I just said about her?"

Emma looked as if her own chin was going to begin wobbling and her eyes suddenly glistened as if hidden tears were forming.

"No," Jason said, afraid that he, too, would start crying.

That was when he heard the doorbell ring.

A moment later, his mother came to the door and said a police detective wanted to talk to him about Alicia Bartlett's murder.

The last person to see Alicia Bartlett alive?

Except for the murderer, of course, Detective Lieutenant Braxton quickly added.

Jason felt himself recoil, as if someone had punched him in the stomach, like the time when he'd collided with Rod Pearson in a game of touch football and had the breath knocked out of him. He had gasped for air, just as he did now, relieved as air rushed into his lungs, not like that other time, lying on the ground, waiting to suffocate and die.

The detective fastened his black eyes upon Jason. His face was thin, as if his flesh had been pulled taut from the back of his head. His eyes were bloodshot. He had refused the cup of tea Jason's mother had offered with an abrupt "Sorry, Mrs. Dorrant. Time is really a factor and I have some important questions for Jason." Turning to Jason, leaning forward, he had said: "I want you to be real careful, Jason, and tell me everything you remember about that last visit with Alicia."

Later, Jason realized that he hadn't told the detective exactly what had happened the afternoon Alicia had died. Not that he had lied. He had told the truth. Under the detective's double-barreled gaze and his rapid-fire questions, Jason had answered as best he could. But he had never been questioned by a detective before and had never had a friend murdered before. The detective also seemed so impatient as he asked his questions that Jason was relieved when he was able to give quick answers.

For instance, when the detective had asked if everything had been normal at Alicia's house that afternoon, Jason had answered unhesitatingly, "Yes." Because everything *had* been normal. Alicia had been fussing and fuming about the jigsaw puzzle as usual, even though she was a whiz at placing the pieces in the right spot. Her brother, Brad, had been a pain in the butt, also as usual, jumping around the swimming pool, pushing and shoving his buddies Greg Chavin and Marv Galehouse, a lot of yelling and screaming. Once in a while, Brad leaped out of the pool, shaking water off his body like a big dog, almost dousing the puzzle, trying to get a rise out of Alicia. Nothing new about that. Brad tried to get a rise out of everybody, although he had spared Jason that particular afternoon. Frankly, Brad was obnoxious. Never sat still. He'd give little pushes to your chest with the flat of his hand as he talked to you, even when he was being friendly. And that was why Jason told the detective that everything was normal that afternoon.

The detective then asked a follow-up question that sounded to Jason like the same question asked in a different way.

"Did Alicia seem upset about anything?"

Jason thought a moment. "Well, she was having trouble with the jigsaw puzzle. It was a hard one, with, like, a thousand pieces. A big red bird, a cardinal."

He told the detective that Alicia had set up a card table on the patio not far from the pool. That was why she had to keep yelling at Brad to stop splashing water all over the place. She'd already filled in the edges of the puzzle, which was the easy part. All the other pieces looked alike to Jason.

The detective looked up from his notebook and shook his head, and Jason could tell he was getting impatient with these details.

"She finally got mad at the puzzle and knocked the pieces off the table, sent them all over the patio," Jason said.

"Did she seem upset about anything other than the puzzle?"

"Well, Brad kept teasing her but he was always teasing her. And everybody else, too."

The detective said nothing. Sat there looking at Jason until Jason began to squirm a bit. He wished he could come up with some big clue to satisfy the detective but there was no big clue that Jason knew of.

"What time did you leave Alicia?" the detective asked.

Jason hesitated. He hadn't been wearing his watch. He never wore a watch during summer vacation because time didn't seem important. "I'm not sure. A few minutes after Brad and his buddies left. I helped Alicia pick up the pieces of the puzzle and we took them and the card table into the house. She offered me a glass of lemonade but I could see she was still not in a very good mood and I came home."

"Did you check the time when you arrived home?"

"Yes," Jason said, pleased to be able to come up with a piece of definite information. "I remember the clock in the front hall striking four as I came in."

"How long did it take you to arrive home from Alicia's house?"

Jason shrugged. "Four or five minutes. She lives right down the street."

Lived, not lives, Jason corrected himself. And the fact of Alicia's death struck him again, but he was determined to hold himself in check, made himself sit stiffly erect.

"See anything suspicious on the street as you walked home?"

"Actually, I didn't walk on the street. I went through the backyards." Proud of himself for being in control. "And I didn't see anybody."

"Alicia was alone in the house when you left?"

"Right. She was headed for the kitchen for lemonade when I said 'See you later.' And came home."

"You said you arrived home at four o'clock. Was anybody else home?"

"No. My mother and sister came home about . . ." He turned to his mother for help.

"Emma and I arrived almost at the same time," his mother said. "Oh, maybe about five or so . . ." She hesitated, frowning. "Why are all these questions so important, Detective?"

"Everything's important, Mrs. Dorrant. And especially Jason's information. We haven't found anyone else who saw her after Jason left her at her house. By tracking Jason's movements and making some kind of timetable, we can trace Alicia's movements. For instance, now we know that Alicia was alone in her house at about four o'clock, when Jason left."

They all sat in silence for a while. Jason glanced at Emma, saw her eyes bright with interest. She had started writing a detective story awhile back and this would provide her with firsthand material.

"Anything else you can tell us, Jason?" the detective asked.

Jason shook his head.

The detective closed his notebook with a snap. All his movements were quick, without wasted effort. "If you think of anything, let us know," he said, rising to his feet.

After he'd left, Jason's mother told him he had done just fine answering the detective's questions. "I know what a strain this must be," she said, touching his cheek.

Heading for his room, Jason wondered whether he had really done just fine, like his mother had said. He flung himself on the bed, trying to sort out his thoughts, trying to recapture exactly what had happened that afternoon. What hadn't he told the detective, and was any of it important, after all?

What he hadn't told: that he wondered whether Alicia was upset about more than the puzzle that afternoon and whether Brad was involved somehow.

He remembered how Alicia kept looking at the pool and yelling at Brad to quiet down. "How the hell can I concentrate with all that noise?" she had yelled.

Hell sounded foreign on her lips. Hell wasn't

exactly a swearword but it was kind of a shock coming from Alicia, who was a proper, dainty little girl.

"What's the matter, Alicia?" Jason had asked. "Are you mad about something?"

"No more than usual," she'd said, pointing with her chin at Brad and his friends. "He gets my dander up."

Jason shook his head in admiration and affection. *Dander.* A grandmother kind of word. That was why he got such a kick out of Alicia. She acted like a little old lady sometimes, as if she'd been born in an earlier time. When most kids spent hours on the Internet, she did jigsaw puzzles. She wore dresses most of the time and was seldom seen in pants or shorts even on hot days. She scolded Brad as if she were his big sister, not his kid sister.

Jason closed his eyes now, remembering how he and Alicia had worked on the puzzle together while trying to ignore the antics going on at the pool. Alicia finally hit her stride and began to place a series of pieces in their proper slots, although she continued to frown and scold.

Brad and his buddies finally abandoned the pool

and toweled themselves off in the sun. Brad wandered over to the patio and stood silhouetted against the sun.

"What would happen, Alicia, if I accidentally tripped and knocked that card table over?" Deliberately stressing the word *accidentally*.

Alicia gave him a withering look. "Haven't you done enough damage today already?" she said in a voice as cold as an icicle, not a kid sister's voice at all.

Brad just stood there, the sun at his back, his face in shadow so that it was impossible to read his expression.

Alicia continued to stare at him as if waiting for a response. "Right?" she said, spitting the word out.

Brad turned away abruptly and joined his friends. The next time Jason looked up they were gone, leaving a heavy silence in their wake.

Alicia muttered something under her breath.

"What did you say?" Jason asked.

"You wouldn't want to know," she said. And that was when she swept her hand across the table and sent the pieces of the puzzle flying in all directions.

She sat there a minute looking at the scattered

pieces. Jason thought she was going to cry. Instead, she said: "I'm tired of doing puzzles. Let's get a cold drink. Mom made some lemonade."

Her lips were trembling and her hands shaking.

Jason's own lips were trembling now as he opened his eyes and stared at the smoke alarm on the ceiling. Should he have gone into all those details with the detective? Or were Alicia and Brad just having another one of their squabbles? Brother-and-sister stuff. Would he have looked stupid if he had told the detective about it and it had turned out to be nothing at all? He had looked stupid too many times in his life. Anyway, did it all really matter? With Alicia dead, that overwhelming knowledge giving him shivers, what did an argument amount to, anyway? Brad was probably sadder than anybody on earth right now, thinking of the lousy way he had treated his sister the day she died. The day she was murdered. Poor Brad, Jason thought. But most of all, poor Alicia.

He didn't try to stop the tears this time. But no tears came. His eyes were dry. And that seemed even worse than crying.

Alvin Dark asked: "What do you have?"

"A suspect," Braxton said.

"What else?"

"A senator who's driving me up a wall. Press and television asking questions I can't answer. A section of town up in arms, that's going to be mad as hell if I . . . we . . . don't come up with something."

The district attorney didn't appear sympathetic as he sipped his coffee. But he did appear relaxed and at ease. Why not? He had managed to abandon headquarters for a few hours of sleep.

"But you have a suspect," Dark said. Sarcastic? Taunting?

"And a gut feeling." Braxton realized the statement probably sounded pathetic but his gut feelings had paid off in the past. And Alvin Dark knew it.

But Dark wasn't giving an inch. "Gut feelings don't hold up before grand juries," he said. "Or in courtrooms. You know what we need."

"Right," Braxton said, feeling like a schoolboy and resenting the hell out of the fact that Dark, two years younger, made him feel like a schoolboy. "Physical evidence."

"Don't you have anything to link the suspect to the crime?" Dark asked. Then, wryly: "Besides that gut feeling."

"Gut feelings have worked in the past. The evidence came later."

"But can you afford to wait till later?"

"What we really need is a confession," Braxton said tentatively.

"From your suspect." Again that touch of sarcasm?

Time for the big move, Braxton thought. And here goes.

"There's an interrogator by the name of Trent. Operates out of a small department up in Vermont.

Has quite a reputation. They say he can get blood out of a stone."

"His name sounds vaguely familiar," Dark said. "Tell me more."

"He conducts seminars all over the place. Answers calls throughout the Northeast. He likes interesting cases. Challenges."

"What makes you think he'll come here?"

"Gibbons," Braxton said. "Gibbons is a law-and-order man. Influential. Chairman of important Senate committees. Someone to hitch your star to. I understand Trent is an ambitious man. I think we can use the senator as bait."

Alvin Dark sipped his coffee. Slowly, deliberately. "I don't like outsiders coming in," he said at last.

"This man's uncanny," Braxton said, doing a sales job. "Part of a new breed of interrogators, trained to extract confessions. He never fails."

Dark was silent, made a great show of finishing his coffee, dabbing his lips with the napkin. He swiveled his chair toward the window. "He's out there. The perp. Killer of a child. Whether he's your suspect or not. That's what bothers me, having a killer out there."

"It bothers me, too," Braxton said, covering his mouth, trying to resist his desperate yawn.

Alvin Dark cracked his knuckles on the table. He liked to think of himself as a man of action. "Okay, call him." Command in his voice as if Braxton were an underling.

"Fine," Braxton said, overlooking the district attorney's superior attitude. The important thing was getting Trent here, not engaging Alvin Dark in a battle of egos. He wanted to turn Trent loose on the boy, get him to admit his guilt. The prospect was almost as sweet as the thought of a good night's sleep.

Trent received the call from Detective Lieutenant George Braxton moments after he had obtained a confession of murder from Adolph Califer, a respected broker who finally admitted that he had strangled his next-door neighbor, with whom he had been carrying on an illicit affair.

Califer had been brilliant during the questioning, parrying Trent's questions with questions of his own or with answers that were not really answers. He had managed to avoid Trent's verbal traps and seemed to take pleasure in it as if an entertaining game were in progress. At times, he not only anticipated the questions but answered them eagerly, so certain was he of his defenses, so confident of his replies.

For a moment or two, Trent had wondered whether Califer would be his first failure. He thought of the reactions of the other cops and detectives in the department, who'd be happy to see him fail. The Highgate Police Department was small, with a roster of only ten full-time officers in charge of a Vermont town near the Canadian border. Trent knew that he was the object of resentment by the other cops. He had never fit the mold from the beginning. Trent had quit college and the pursuit of a degree in psychology to fulfill a childhood dream: becoming a cop. He had continued taking courses as he went from beat cop to the detective squad, in a career that wasn't spectacular but was nevertheless successful, particularly in the questioning of witnesses and suspects. The population of Highgate swelled during the winter skiing season and Trent had made his mark when he obtained a confession to four gruesome murders from a serial killer. The resulting headlines had established Trent's reputation.

He found himself on call from other departments.

He polished his techniques, studied all kinds of interrogative methods and ultimately developed his own system. He conducted occasional seminars and envisioned breaking away entirely from police work and the unending litany of confessions. He was aware that he was waiting for the right case to come along.

Meanwhile, there was Califer.

Focusing on him, Trent began to tire of the cat-and-mouse moves. He had an ace up his sleeve. But the trick was to play it at the right time, to be patient, to await the proper moment.

So he allowed Califer to conduct his game of interrogative hide-and-seek. Interrogations called for flexibility and subtlety within the rules and regulations that Trent had developed. And, at times, a waiting game had to be played with patience as the watchword. Whatever weapons Trent had at his disposal had to be brought into play when it was psychologically right. The weapons, of course, consisted of information that the subject didn't know Trent possessed. Or, most often, knowledge of the subject that Trent had detected during the questioning itself.

At a moment when Califer was off guard and thus vulnerable, Trent made the decisive move.

"What was your daughter's name?" he asked, quite innocently, almost casually.

Stunned, Califer turned away, averting his eyes for the first time during the interrogation. When he looked at Trent again, he couldn't disguise his astonishment. Trent saw Califer's defenses begin to crumble.

"She's dead," Califer said, voice flat with resignation, shoulders slumping, chin dropping to his chest.

"I know," Trent said, making his voice soothing and sympathetic, one of many voices he employed during his confrontations with suspects.

"She was only five when she died," Califer said, voice breaking now.

Trent had not only waited for the proper moment to spring the question but had attacked Califer from the inside, not the outside, touching the one vital spot where Califer was vulnerable.

Ten minutes later, Califer confessed.

And five minutes after that, Trent received the call from Detective Lieutenant George Braxton.

"I'm calling from Monument down in Massachusetts," Braxton said. "We need your services here. Desperately."

"And why's that?" Trent asked dryly, knowing the answer, of course.

"The town's in an uproar over the murder of a child. We have a suspect who needs interrogation. Can you help us?"

Carl Seaton and Califer, all within six days. He didn't need another so soon.

"How did you reach me?" he asked, knowing that he was stalling, that he never could resist an appeal to his expertise.

"Your department in Highgate gave us your number in Rutland. I've been standing by until you wrapped up your current interrogation. Congratulations. I understand you scored another one."

Braxton's congratulations rang hollow but the words still pleased him. Trent knew, however, where Braxton's real interest lay. Sure enough, Braxton immediately proved him right. "Can you come?"

"Where's Monument?" Trent asked, but only going through the motions, really.

"Central Massachusetts. About four hours from

Highgate." Trent heard him pause. "Senator Gibbons is interested in the case. He said to call this to your attention. His grandson knew the victim. They were in the second grade together."

Braxton had played his ace and Trent's interest quickened. The senator was a man of powerful authority and influence. He was an advocate of tough anticrime laws. A good man to have in your corner.

"Details," Trent said.

He heard the relief in Braxton's voice as he recited the details of a too-familiar situation. The murdered girl, the tension-filled town, the suspect.

"He's more than a suspect. Someone we feel is the perp. Twelve-year-old neighbor of the victim," Braxton added.

"Evidence?"

"That's the hitch. No physical evidence. No witnesses. No weapon. No fingerprints. That's why we're calling you. We have a suspect who fits the profile. But we need a confession. Otherwise, he walks."

"Is the scenario in place?" Trent asked. The answer to this question would determine whether he would accept the assignment.

No hesitation on Braxton's part. "Yes. The scenario's in place. We know about your work with Fallow and Blake."

Trent frowned at the mention of Blake. Blake had been an aberration with a predisposition to confessing.

"Arrangements?"

"Senator Gibbons will provide transportation. He'll have a driver at your disposal. Pick you up anywhere at any time."

"How much time will I have with the suspect?"

"Three hours. Maybe four."

"Parents?"

"Father's away on a business trip. We anticipate that the mother will accept the scenario."

Trent's mind still echoed from the Ping-Pong-like questioning session with Califer and his too-smooth, too-confident voice and the effort it had taken to break him down. He had a sudden urge to reject this new assignment. *But do I want to be a small-town cop all my life?* How could he turn his back on a case that would leave a powerful senator in his debt?

"Fax me the details," Trent said, giving Braxton

the number. "Everything. Spell it out. I don't want to have to read between the lines. And I don't like surprises later."

"Right," Braxton said.

"And have your driver pick me up in Highgate at six sharp in the morning."

"Right," said Braxton again.

Trent hung up the phone, despising himself for allowing a politician to influence his decision. But then Trent had despised himself for quite a long time, anyway.

Jason was surprised when he entered police headquarters to find a normal place that could have been any business office in Monument. He'd expected telephones to be ringing wildly, a bank of monitors showing all kinds of activity, police officers coming and going, and cigar-smoking detectives in plain clothes hunched over their desks, like on television or in the movies.

Instead, Jason found himself in a small cubicle occupied by a gray-haired man in a crisp white shirt and blue tie sitting at a desk behind a plate-glass window. The place was so quiet that Jason could hear the humming of the air conditioner.

The officer, whose name was Henry Kendall and who had accompanied Jason to police headquarters, nodded at the man at the desk. The man apparently pushed a hidden button that buzzed a door open to their left. Officer Kendall led Jason to another office that was as bare and barren as the principal's outer office at school. No pictures on the walls, no desks or chairs, no curtains on the windows.

"The others will be here in a minute or two," Officer Kendall said, voice soft and gentle. "You're going to be a big help to the investigation, Jason. You'll do just fine."

After he'd left, Jason shivered slightly in the coolness of the room. He walked to the window and looked out at Main Street. Traffic moved slowly as if the heat had affected even the cars and trucks. People walked languidly as if in slow motion. Jason thought of his mother and wondered if coming here was a mistake. Then wondered why he should be having that thought.

He had been surprised earlier that morning when he glanced outside his bedroom window and saw a police cruiser pulling into the driveway. Another visit from the police? His breath quickened and his heart accelerated. An emergency of some kind? But the blue and white lights on the roof of the cruiser weren't flashing and the big red-faced officer who got out of it strolled leisurely up the driveway toward the front door.

Hearing the chime of the doorbell, Jason stood still, urging his heart to calm down if that was possible. The sight of the policeman brought back the image of Alicia Bartlett as he had last seen her at her house. *Last seen her*. Poor Alicia.

"Jason."

His mother's voice reached him as if from far away.

A moment later, Jason stood in the foyer with his mother and the police officer.

"This is Officer Kendall," his mother explained to Jason. "He's asking for your help in the investigation."

"Actually, we're asking several people for their help," the officer explained.

"A detective spoke to Jason yesterday," his mother said. "For quite a long time."

"I know, Mrs. Dorrant," the officer said, his

voice surprisingly gentle for such a big man. "But this is a new approach we're trying. We have some special interrogators down at headquarters who will be asking people who were out on the street on Monday what they might have seen."

"But I already told the detective that I didn't see anything," Jason said, and instantly regretted having spoken. Saying those words would probably eliminate him from the questioning and he really wanted to be part of the investigation.

"We realize that, Jason," the policeman said. "But these experts can really get people thinking about what they might have seen. Sometimes you've actually seen things that you don't realize you've seen. Or heard things that you didn't think were important at that time. With the right kind of questioning, evidence can turn up that didn't seem to be evidence. . . ."

Jason sighed with relief when his mother said: "Well, I'm sure Jason would like to help. He's a good kid."

"Fine," Officer Kendall said. "I can drive him to headquarters now, where he'll join the others."

"How long will this take?" Jason's mother asked.

"Oh, maybe a couple, three hours. We'll drive him back when it's all over."

Jason's mother frowned, doubt appearing in her eyes. "My husband's out of town, won't be back until tomorrow."

What's that got to do with anything? Jason wondered, afraid that his mother might change her mind about letting him go.

The officer frowned, too. "We're doing all we can to find who did this terrible thing to that little girl."

His voice was so gentle and kind that Jason wondered if he ever got up the nerve to arrest anybody.

Jason's mother nodded. "Well, I guess it's important for him to do his part," she said. But she seemed skeptical. "How many other people are involved?" she asked.

"Four, maybe five. Mostly young people because they happened to be out on the street Monday. Jason probably knows them." He glanced at his watch. "It's important to move fast because time is a factor."

"I'd rather go with him," she said, still reluctant,

"but Emma's got a doctor appointment in half an hour and they're always booked so full . . ." She looked at him anxiously and Jason blew air, impatient to be on his way. The officer glanced at his watch again.

"Well, okay," she said, "do your best, Jason." To Officer Kendall she said: "He's been upset by all this."

This time, it was Jason's turn to frown. "Aw, Ma," he said.

And she smiled wanly.

"Be on your way, then," she said.

And here he was, in this barren office, wondering if his mother was right to be worried. He hadn't seen anything unusual. He would probably be revealed as a fake.

The doors swung open and Officer Kendall was back with two guys Jason recognized. Jack O'Shea and Tim Connors. Jocks. They usually wore turned-around baseball caps, always passing a basketball between them. No baseball caps or basketball now, although they came into the room in that loose-limbed jiggling walk typical of jocks. They were followed by a kid named Danny Edison who sometimes sat at the same cafeteria table with Jason. Danny was a thin intense kid, face raw with acne.

Jason was glad to see Jimmy Orlando appear. Jimmy was a normal kid. Not a jock, not a major brain. Just a regular kid. Like what Jason hoped others saw when they looked at him.

Officer Kendall said: "Lieutenant Braxton will be here in a minute and give you fellows the low-down on everything. He's in charge of the investigation."

After he left the room, they all stood around awkwardly. The two jocks meandered toward the window and huddled together like conspirators. Jimmy pulled a paperback book from his pocket and, leaning against a wall, started reading.

Danny approached Jason and they looked at each other for a moment.

"This is kind of neat, isn't it?" Danny said, almost whispering. "I mean, being part of an investigation and everything."

Jason nodded, glad to be talking to somebody.

"What do you think's going to happen?" Jason asked.

"I don't know. Give statements. I hope we don't have to write anything down, like an essay. I'm rotten at composition."

"Maybe they'll record our answers," Jason said. "And all we have to do is talk."

They fell silent. The jocks continued to confer at the window but glanced now and then at Danny and Jason. Jimmy turned a page of his book but Jason had a feeling that he wasn't really reading.

"Don't you feel, like, kind of weird?" Danny asked.

"Right," Jason said. "Because I don't know what I'm going to say. I mean, I didn't see anything unusual that day."

Danny shook his head. "I mean, about Alicia Bartlett. That you were the last person to see her alive."

Jason frowned in surprise. He hadn't realized that his visit with Alicia on Monday had become common knowledge. *Is that why he's talking to me?* Jason wondered. *Curious, looking for inside information?*

"*One* of the last to see her alive," Jason amended.

Danny lowered his eyes. When he blushed, his

acne seemed to come alive, the rawness of the zits emphasized.

"Sorry," he said. "That's what I meant."

At the same time, Jason became aware of the jocks looking his way, their eyes lingering on him. He grew uneasy. He didn't like to have attention focused on him. That was why he never raised his hand in class. He could feel his own cheeks getting warm, glad that he had been spared acne, at least. Had *everyone* heard about him and Alicia Bartlett?

Silence again. Jimmy Orlando closed his book and remained leaning against the wall. The jocks again turned their backs on the room and looked out the window. Danny seemed to be staring at something over Jason's shoulder. The room suddenly became colder, as if the air-conditioning had been turned up.

Finally, the door swung open and Lieutenant Braxton stepped in. Still thin and intense, as if he were made of wire instead of bones and muscle.

"I'm Lieutenant Braxton and we're ready to get started, guys," he said in his brisk, businesslike way. "We really appreciate your cooperation and hope that we can come up with some vital information, information that you don't even know you have."

He looked at each of them in turn and his eyes finally rested on Jason. He gave no sign of recognition.

"Here's how it works." He took a notepad out of his jacket pocket and flipped it open. Eyes on the pad, he said: "Experts at interrogation will be questioning you. Two of you, John O' Shea and Timothy Connors, will be questioned simultaneously because you were together most of that day. The others will be questioned individually." Looking up, he said: "Time is of the essence, gentlemen, so let's get started." Consulting the pad again, he said: "First up is Jason Dorrant."

He directed his eyes to Jason, recognizing him for the first time. "Okay, Jason, I'll take you along to your expert." To the others, he said: "I'll be right back."

Jason followed Lieutenant Braxton out of the office, wondering again if he had made a mistake coming here.

When Trent stepped into the limousine, immersing himself in the sudden flood of air-conditioning, he was surprised to find a young woman seated inside.

"My name is Sarah Downes and I'm with the district attorney's office in Wickburg," she announced. "Lieutenant Braxton asked me to ride down to Monument with you and provide you with background information."

"That was kind of Braxton," Trent said, disguising his dismay and his irritation. He didn't enjoy surprises, either in his private life or in his interrogations. He had anticipated a long quiet ride, alone with his thoughts, reviewing the procedures that lay ahead. Yet he supposed a personal briefing now would save time later. And time was always a factor with interrogations.

"Your reputation precedes you," Sarah Downes said. "I've read your transcripts and listened to your tapes. They've helped my own interrogations." She hesitated, as if she wanted to say more, then decided not to.

"Thank you," Trent said, settling back as the limo moved smoothly forward, the tinted windows sealing them off from the rest of the world. The driver was a dark shadow at the wheel behind a glass partition.

"Braxton said to tell you that they're all set to carry out the scenario. The suspect is being taken to police headquarters along with four other neighborhood boys. Under the pretext, of course, that they're helping the investigation. The suspect will be isolated for you. All of this timed with your arrival."

Something in her voice, a tone, an inflection, that he could not immediately pin down, caused him to glance at her. Devoid of makeup, except for a faint pink lipstick, wearing a gray career suit, white blouse. Everything about her understated and elegant. Thirty years old, give or take a year or two. Attractive in a subdued unflamboyant way.

Trent felt old beside her. Her freshness and crispness in contrast to his own—what? Not only age, although he was maybe ten or fifteen years older. All the confessions, all those terrible acts he had listened to, that had somehow become a part of him, that separated them more than the years. Entire worlds separated them.

"Give me some background," Trent said.

"You read the fax. Braxton is very thorough."

"I'd like to hear it from you. Tell me about the suspect."

"His name, as you know, is Jason Dorrant. He's twelve years old. Shy, somewhat introverted. No previous arrests. But he attacked a classmate last year in the school cafeteria. Apparently unprovoked. He knew the victim, lived on the same street, was one of the last people—if not the last—to see her alive. Braxton is convinced that he's the perpetrator."

That tone of voice again, the hint of doubt. Trent's instincts were seldom wrong—that was why he had scored so many successes. And he allowed his instincts to lead him now as he asked, "And you?"

She looked at him in surprise. "Me?"

"Yes, are you convinced the boy's the perpetrator?"

"What I think doesn't matter," she said.

"Yes, it does," Trent replied. "Everything matters. And I have to know everything that's possible to know before I proceed."

She shrugged. "All right, I admit that I'm somewhat doubtful. There is absolutely no physical evidence. Nothing to link the boy to the crime scene. And I wonder whether Braxton is yielding to pressure. The town, the senator. Acting too quickly . . ."

"Any other suspects?"

"Not really. Family members are always questioned, of course. But the father, mother and brother all can account for their time and movements. Father at the office, mother shopping with a friend. The brother, a boy named Brad, thirteen years old, was with two friends the entire afternoon. No other leads. That leaves us with Jason Dorrant." A wisp of hair had loosened, falling across her forehead. She swept it back. "I'm uneasy about the situation, about this boy, Jason."

"You're overlooking one thing, Ms. Downes."

"What's that?"

"The interrogation."

Her face tightened, her cheeks becoming taut.

"Don't you think the interrogation will bring out the truth?" Trent asked.

She sighed, turning to him. "It should." Then that shrug again. "But . . ."

"But what?"

As if she'd made a sudden decision, she turned and looked at him directly. "You're in the business of obtaining confessions," she said. "That's why you're being brought in. That's what bothers me."

"Don't you think I'm also looking for the truth?" he asked. "That the truth comes out of the interrogation?"

"Not always," she said. "The Blake case, and Abbott. Both confessions recanted . . ."

"But upheld by the courts," he countered. "It's hard to deny what's on the record, the spoken word . . ."

And now Trent knew what disturbed him about Sarah Downes, beyond her doubts about his interrogations. Somehow, she reminded him of Lottie. Not on the surface. Sarah Downes was cool and poised and elegant. Lottie had been disorganized, often in disarray, particularly after a few margaritas with her friends. She had also been warm and affectionate toward everyone, from stray kittens to old men on park benches.

But the skepticism, the doubt in Sarah Downes's voice and manner echoed Lottie and that last sad conversation with her the night before she died.

"I don't know you anymore," Lottie had said. "Who are you, anyway?"

And because she'd obviously been drinking, Trent answered lightly: "What you see is what you get."

"I'm not sure what I see," Lottie retorted, alert suddenly, eyes flashing, voice crisp and flat.

Taken aback by the lightning change in her manner, Trent thought of his days and nights away from home, time spent at the department, on the road for interrogations, the endless pursuit of the right answers. He saw how much he had neglected her, having assumed that she was content with her volunteer work at the animal shelter, her afternoon drinks with friends, the books in which she immersed herself.

"But, wait," she said, "I do know who you are."

Voice rising as if she'd made a startling discovery. "You are an interrogator. That's what you do. And you are what you do."

You are what you do.

Like an accusation.

That had been their last conversation. She'd been asleep when he went to bed after studying his notes for the Lane case and still sleeping soundly when he left for headquarters early the next morning. By nightfall, he stood beside her hospital bed in a hopeless vigil. She had been the victim of a freak accident, a minor collision of automobiles in which the air bag and seat belt conspired to cause her death—trapped by safety devices suddenly turned lethal. Lottie died during the night, without regaining consciousness. Thus began the period of mourning from that day to this, eighteen months later, mourning the lost years ahead they might have shared and the past years that had been wasted.

You are what you do. Her final indictment of him.

He shook off these thoughts, bringing himself gratefully back to the limo, the landscape passing muted and surrealistic outside the tinted window. And Sarah Downes sitting beside him, legs crossed now, one foot in the sensible low-heeled shoe swinging back and forth, back and forth.

Body language. At which Trent had made himself adept for his interrogations. The small clues of movement, the use of hands and feet, the body tense or relaxed, leaning forward or drawing away, the attitude of the chin and the trembling of eyelids, all the telltale signs. What clues did Sarah Downes now supply? That swinging foot, her folded arms guarding her chest, the small beat of the pulse in her temple.

"Tell me about the victim," Trent said. "The child."

"Alicia Bartlett. Seven years old," she said, sighing. "Precocious. But a nice little girl. Polite and well bred. Excellent grades in school. Utterly feminine. Loved her American Girl doll Amanda. Hobby: jigsaw puzzles, even in this day of computer games. She and Jason Dorrant worked at a puzzle during that last visit."

Trent conjured up pictures of twelve-year-old Jason Dorrant with seven-year-old Alicia Bartlett, heads bent together as they worked over a jigsaw puzzle. They, too, were a puzzle to be solved.

Sarah Downes's swinging foot now stopped.

Trent waited. Finally she said: "I wonder . . ." Then faltered, shifted her body and fell silent.

"And what do you wonder, Ms. Downes?" His voice light, but not playful, suspecting a revealing remark.

"First, you can call me Sarah, since we'll be working together."

Trent withdrew a bit. He had admitted no one into his privacy, had avoided intimacy since Lottie's death. No first-name greetings, no first name given. He wanted to operate alone, travel light. Yet he wanted somehow to convince this young woman that he was more than just an interrogator, not some sort of monster who neglected the human condition of his subjects and their victims.

"All right, Sarah," he said, conceding her name but withholding his own. "What do you wonder about?"

"How you can stand it. All those confessions. I've often wondered how priests handle it, sitting in the dark, listening to all the sins, all the foul things people do to each other."

The foul things.

I must lie down where all the ladders start,
In the foul rag-and-bone shop of the heart.

The old poem which had become a sort of credo through the years.

He said the words aloud but almost to himself: " 'Down where all the ladders start, in the foul rag-and-bone shop of the heart.' "

"Yeats," she said.

Gratified that she recognized the poem, he said: "I admit that I have sleepless nights. Or I wake up from dreams I can't remember except that terrible things happened in them. All of it, I suppose, from what I've heard in the interrogations. But you learn to live in isolation. And that's where the trouble lies." What was he admitting to this young woman that he had never admitted even to Lottie? "The terrible thing is that the priest can give absolution. Absolve the sinners. Send them on their way with a clean heart. I can only listen and turn the confession into an indictment. And go on my own way . . ."

"To another case, another interrogation."

He nodded in agreement.

"And that's enough for you?"

You are what you do.

Or should I be more than that?

The limo swerved, and he and Sarah Downes were almost thrown against each other, shoulders touching, the faint scent of her cologne reaching him, like a soft breeze in a leafy glade, the echo of an old song coming into his mind.

"Sorry," came the word from the speaker connected to the driver. "A dog in the road . . ."

Sarah Downes drew away, a wan smile on her face.

"I guess I've envied you for a long time," she said. "Wanted to be as expert, as efficient . . ." Her voice trailed off.

"But now you're not sure," he suggested.

She turned her eyes on him, said nothing.

What did he see in those deep gray eyes? Pity, perhaps? Or revulsion? And which was worse?

An unaccountable sadness settled on him, along with the familiar exhaustion that he wore like an old suit, as the limo continued on its way to Monument.

Lieutenant Braxton greeted Trent at the rear door of police headquarters. As the detective introduced himself, Trent took in the wiry intensity of the man. Tall and thin, all sharp angles, cheekbones and chin, shoulder blades sharp in the sweat-stained white shirt.

"Glad you're here," Braxton said, voice brisk. His handshake was also brisk. And brief. "No time to waste," he said. "Sarah Downes filled in the cracks." Not a question but a statement that required no answer.

Sarah had quietly drifted away after a curt nod to both men.

"Let's go," Braxton commanded, turning abruptly toward the hallway.

Trent disliked being hurried and purposely lagged behind. Braxton stopped and looked over his shoulder at him. "The senator would like a word with you."

At the same moment, Senator Gibbons stepped into the hallway. He looked as if he had just emerged from a political cartoon, everything about him spectacular, almost a caricature. A shock of white hair, bulbous nose, wide smile and gleaming buck teeth. But he carried himself with an air of authority that contradicted the exaggerations.

Trent expected a booming hearty greeting but Senator Gibbons shook hands with a gentleness that surprised him.

"Thank God you're here," he said breathlessly. "The suspect's waiting and we know you'll do your best, Trent. The town needs an arrest, families are upset." He hesitated, frowning, then added: "Including my own." An obvious reference to his grandson's friendship with the victim. "We're counting on you, Trent, and I will owe you much if you can see this through. You can write your own ticket." He paused, for dramatic effect, Trent supposed. "I keep my promises."

Trent had no illusions about campaign promises. However, this was not a campaign but an investigation in which the senator was personally involved.

Braxton, who had been moving impatiently at the senator's side, said: "Let me show you the office."

Trent's pulse quickened, his old enthusiasm for the pursuit of the confession renewed and revitalized, the game of thrust and parry accelerating his breathing.

The office to which Braxton led him was perfect. Small and cluttered and claustrophobic. No windows, which eliminated the necessity of drawing the shades. No lamps on the desks, the light coming directly and harshly from a ceiling bulb. No air-conditioning, either. Trent, in fact, felt a slight wafting of heat as he entered the room. Two desks and a filing cabinet took up most of the space, which meant that he and the suspect would be in close proximity, their knees almost touching as they sat in the two chairs arranged opposite each other. That was the intent, of course, to conduct the interrogation in a small space with no room for the suspect to be comfortable.

"Okay?" Braxton asked, a frown on his face. Did he ever relax? Trent wondered.

"Okay," he echoed. "Exactly what I need."

"We had the extra desk brought in to make it more crowded."

"Perfect."

"You'll note that one chair is higher than the other as you requested. Need water? Snacks?"

"Nothing like that. Austerity. No refreshments."

"Fine," Braxton said, with a small sigh of satisfaction.

"How much time do I have?" Trent asked.

"The mother was a bit doubtful but not really suspicious," Braxton said, leaning back against the doorjamb, seemingly relaxed for the first time. "Her husband's away until tomorrow. I'd say you've got three hours, minimum. She may become curious after that and either call or visit."

"The other young people?"

"It's hard to fake long interrogations. We may

have to let them go after an hour or so. Hard to predict. The quicker you can work, the better."

"It all depends, of course," Trent said.

Glancing around the room one more time, Trent sighed. Carl Seaton, Califer and now this boy, all in the space of a week. But a twelve-year-old boy should be easy enough to handle. He thought of Senator Gibbons and his words—*you can write your own ticket*—which provided the necessary thrust of energy he needed.

"Bring in the suspect," he said.

The boy. Pausing at the doorway before entering the office. On the thin side, black hair neatly combed, blue plaid shirt open at the collar, sharply creased chinos.

Trent imagined the boy's mother inspecting him prior to his departure for headquarters, checking his fingernails, perhaps. Checking the fingernails himself as they shook hands, Trent found that there was no evidence of their having been bitten. An indication. Everything was an indication.

Trent ushered him into the office. The boy's step was halting, blue eyes blinking in the harsh light. He appeared intimidated, which was to be expected, a glint of curiosity in his eyes, but no suspicion. Trent was expert at detecting suspicion.

Arranging a smile on his face, he welcomed the boy with a raising of his arms, an attitude of praise for something not yet earned.

"You're Jason?" Omitting the family name, establishing a sense of familiarity but maintaining a degree of authority for himself, announcing only his own family name. "I'm Trent."

He motioned to the boy to be seated, maneuvering deftly so that the boy ended up in the lower chair. Trent seated himself opposite, slouching a bit so that his loftier appearance would not be obvious until later and even then almost subliminally.

"I appreciate your cooperation, Jason. And will try to make this as brief and as painless as possible. It would be wonderful if you came up with information that would help find the perpetrator of this terrible crime." Voice mild, informal.

The boy nodded. "I hope I can help. I'll do my best."

His first words. Well-modulated voice. A small swallow before answering. Hands moving slightly but not defensively.

"I know you will."

Jason shot a quick glance around the room, observing it for the first time.

"Sorry for the smallness of the office," Trent said. "All the rooms are being used and we drew this one." The use of *we* designed to give the boy a sense of their being in this together, as partners, as associates.

Nodding again, Jason seemed to relax, settling back a bit in the chair.

Trent positioned his hand over the Record button of the tape recorder. "For the purpose of accuracy, we'll be recording our conversation. Is this acceptable, Jason?"

The boy nodded in agreement.

Trent looked at the boy's trusting face, the surface innocence in his wide-eyed gaze. Was he truly innocent or was this a mask? Trent was aware of the masks people wear and it was his job to remove the masks, if not entirely, then at least to allow a glimpse of the evil underneath. Was there evil in this boy? Was he capable of an evil act? We are all capable, Trent thought, remembering Carl Seaton and the innocence in his eyes, which resembled the look in the eyes of Jason Dorrant.

"Just relax, Jason. Think of this as a conversation, no more, no less." Trent was conscious of using his avuncular voice. "We'll talk about the events of Monday. What you saw and what you remember seeing." He was conscious of avoiding the word *murder,* would use soft words throughout the interrogation. "Memory is a strange device, Jason." The constant use of Jason's name was important, personal, avoiding the impersonal. "It plays tricks. What we remember or think we remember. And the opposite, what we've forgotten or think we've forgotten. We'll find out about it all together." Establishing them as a team. "Think of this as a kind of adventure."

"I *hope* I can help out," the boy said.

"Don't worry about it. Just relax. We're alone here. Only the two of us. You don't mind being alone, away from the rest of your friends, do you?"

And now the first important step.

"I mean, we can have other people here, if you want. A lawyer or counsel. Or even your mother."

The object was to isolate the boy, to avoid the presence of a lawyer or parent or guardian. It had to be done immediately at the outset and so deftly that the boy would not become suspicious. The words were important, of course, because they would appear on the official record—audio and transcript—but what would not show up on the record was Trent's casual attitude, the shrug of his shoulders that conveyed the ridiculous idea of having other people present. The mention of his mother was deliberate, counting on the boy's preadolescent pride—the humiliation of having his mother on hand to give him support—all of this to elicit from the boy the answer he sought and now received.

"No, that's fine."

And to make certain:

"Okay, this way then, without counsel?"

"Yes."

"Fine, Jason. Then let's proceed. First of all, tell me a bit about yourself."

"Well, I'm twelve years old, thirteen in November. I'll be starting eighth grade in September."

Jason fell silent. What else was there to tell?

"Hobbies?"

Jason shrugged. "I'm not too interested in hobbies. I read sometimes. E-mail on the Internet. I have a pen pal in Australia. He lives in Melbourne."

"Chat rooms on the Internet?"

"There's a teen chat room. But I only listen. Watch. I mean, I never say anything."

"Shy, right?"

An inclination of the head. "I guess so."

"Spend a lot of time alone?"

"Kind of. I have a little sister. Her name's Emma. She's a nice kid, smart."

"Friends?"

"Not many. I guess I don't make friends too easy."

Jason was impatient to get on with the questions about Monday, even though he didn't think he had much to offer and would probably disappoint this Mr. Trent. He was also uncomfortable with these personal questions. What did they have to do with what he had seen or not seen that day? Maybe Mr. Trent was trying to find out how reliable he would be as a witness. The questions also made Jason realize how empty his life really was. The guys in the other rooms probably had a lot of things to tell— Jack O'Shea and Tim Connors could brag about the basketball games they won, for instance. What did he have to offer? An e-mail pen pal from Australia. *I read sometimes.*

"What kind of books do you like to read?" Mr. Trent asked, as if reading his mind.

"All kinds. But I like mysteries. Horror stories. Stephen King. Science fiction."

"You don't mind all that violence in those books? People killing each other?"

"It's only stories. They're not real."

"How about movies and television? Do you like violent ones, too? Horror stuff?"

Jason was puzzled. He liked horror stories but he wasn't wild about them and somehow these questions made it sound like he was some kind of fanatic when it came to horror stuff.

"I like other kinds of stories and movies, too. I mean, adventure. Like *Indiana Jones,* and *Star Wars.*"

"They're kind of violent, too, aren't they?"

"I don't know." He thought of them as cartoons, unrelated to anything in real life. "They're unreal."

"You seem to be fascinated by things that are unreal," Trent said.

Do I? Jason wondered. He had never really thought about it.

"Do you sometimes get confused between what's real and unreal?"

Jason squirmed, fidgeted, tried not to show his impatience and his growing uneasiness.

"I don't know what you mean," he said.

He felt like he did in class when the teacher explained something that he didn't understand, unable to process it in his mind. That was what was happening now with this real-unreal stuff.

"I mean, are you always aware of what is real—what is happening to you at any given moment—or maybe what's not real, but fantasy? Like a dream? Do you sometimes confuse a dream with what's actually going on?"

"No." Emphatic. Why was he asking these questions?

Trent wanted to move on. The boy's attitude, his restlessness, his hands moving to his face, scratching at his arm, all indicated his innocence and his puzzlement. But his disposition toward violent movies and stories was now on the record for whatever use might be made of it later.

Not wishing to make the boy uncomfortable, Trent changed tactics.

"Now, let's get down to the business about Monday, the day you worked on that puzzle with Alicia."

Avoiding the fact that that was the day of Alicia's murder.

Almost eagerly, Jason nodded.

"Tell me about that day, Jason. Your activities in a general way, and then we can get down to specifics and I'll help you remember what you think you don't remember. Regard it as a kind of game, okay?"

"Sure." Relief in his voice.

And Jason told him. How he spent the day, from the time he got up and ate breakfast and went to the Y with his mother, lunchtime, cheeseburgers, and the afternoon, visiting Alicia at her house and the jigsaw puzzle. Then home. Exactly what he had told the detective.

Trent listened, his eyes and his ears alert to the boy's voice, his postures and attitudes, taking note of the way the movement of his body either matched or clashed with his narrative. That was why Trent finished the interrogations in such exhaustion, of both mind and body, all his senses concentrating on the subject, absorbing, accumulating details and nuances, impressions.

And now to move into a new phase of questioning.

"How were you feeling Monday?"

"How was I feeling?" Surprised, puzzled.

"Yes. Were you happy or sad or upset about something?"

Again, Jason felt disquiet and unease, like something was wrong.

"These are funny questions," he said. "About how I was feeling, I mean. Did the way I was feeling affect what I saw and did that day?"

A red light beamed in Trent's mind. The boy was only deceptively docile and naive. He would have to proceed more carefully.

"Well, if you were worried about something, for instance, it might provide a distraction. So that you wouldn't be as sharp with your observations."

"I see," the boy said. "But no, I wasn't upset. In fact, I was kind of happy, I guess you'd call it. I mean, school was over. No more classes, no more homework. Yeah, I guess I was happy. Would that be a distraction?"

"Maybe. We'll see."

The boy looked doubtful again.

"Now, let's go over it once more. At first, you said you saw nobody that afternoon. We've narrowed down the time of possible observations as the afternoon, after lunch, two periods of time, actually. Prior to the time you spent with Alicia and afterward. The period when you were on your way to her house and the period when you were on your way home. The first period—who did you see, whom did you meet?"

Jason had become aware of how hot the office had gotten, a gathering of heat that seemed to grow in intensity as the questioning went on. He was also aware of how close to him Mr. Trent sat, their knees almost touching. Also, had Mr. Trent suddenly grown taller? He seemed taller now than when Jason had first entered the room, seemed to loom over him. Besides all this, Jason was filled with a sense of failure. He had not seen anyone suspicious.

"Like I told you before, I didn't see anyone suspicious."

"But, Jason, we don't know yet what a suspicious person would look like. I'm not talking about some stranger lurking at the mouth of an alley. We've established that you don't remember seeing anyone like that. But what I'm looking for is something of a dubious nature. For instance, take a druggist. Someone familiar you've done business with in his store, a pharmacy. He's not suspicious in himself. But suppose you saw him out of context from the pharmacy."

Seeing the puzzlement on the boy's face, he explained. "Let's say that you saw him outside the drugstore at a time when he should be in the store. Say you saw him suddenly hurrying through the park. Then a man who was not himself suspicious would suddenly become a questionable figure because of where he was at the moment, or what he was doing at that particular moment. That's what I am searching for.

"So, tell me whom you saw that afternoon on the way to Alicia's house."

Jason felt more confident now. He would tell Mr. Trent exactly what he saw and let him decide whether there was anything suspicious about it.

"Well, I saw a mailman. I don't know his name, but I've seen him a lot. He doesn't deliver the mail on our street but to stores and business places on Main Street. He was delivering mail as usual."

"Where did you see him?"

"Going into the building between the real estate

office and the place next door with all the copy machines and printing stuff. He was carrying a bunch of letters and envelopes."

"Not out of context, then?" Testing to be sure that the boy had perceived the meaning of *context*.

"Right. Just where you'd expect him to be, doing what you'd expect him to be doing."

"Excellent," Trent said.

And Jason smiled with satisfaction. For once, he had provided the right answer, even though he knew it had led nowhere and certainly hadn't helped the investigation.

"Who else?" Trent asked, disguising his impatience with these particular queries.

"Well, a couple of kids from school."

"Were they alone or together? I mean, did you see them individually, or separately?"

"Well, two of them were pushing their bikes. One of the bikes had a flat tire. They were kids from school but I don't know their names. . . ."

"Younger than you? Or the same age?"

"Younger, like in the fourth or fifth grade, maybe."

And suddenly, Jason drew in his breath sharply

as an idea occurred to him, stunning in its audacity. At the same moment, he saw Mr. Trent's eyes narrow, as if he had somehow *seen* the idea forming in Jason's mind. What Jason had been thinking, what had taken his breath away, was this: He could make up someone, someone suspicious. He could pretend he had spotted a stranger in town after all. Maybe a strange kid he had never seen before. Someone to satisfy this Mr. Trent. To show that he had been alert.

Yet, at the same time, Jason knew that he had never been a good liar. He blushed easily, a pulse beating dangerously in his temples whenever he tried to fake someone out. Like sometimes pretending he had done his homework or telling his mother and father that he had no homework at all. In school, when teachers swept their eyes around the room, searching for suspicious activity, Jason would immediately begin to blush, afraid that he looked guilty even though he wasn't. So how could he possibly lie to this man whose eyes were so penetrating, who often looked at Jason as if he could see right inside his brain, as he was doing at this minute? Jason looked away, dropped his eyes, acknowledging that he simply could not lie, could not pretend that he had seen what he had not seen.

Trent, too, experienced a moment of revelation, a flash of—what?—in the boy's eyes. Faster than the blinking of an eye, the boy had revealed something hidden and furtive that he brought out to the surface of his mind for a quick look and then dismissed. Something he remembered, perhaps? And then discarded? Or something else? A revelation of some sort? Or a sudden planned deception? Trent noted that during that brief flash, the boy's body underwent a change, went suddenly into a defensive posture, stiff, taut. Something had happened inside the boy, like a fault line moving below the surface. A warning light went on in Trent's mind.

"What is it?" he asked.

"What?" The boy startled now, a look of apprehension crossing his face, his eyes darting fearfully.

"It's not smart to be deceptive, Jason. We have to trust each other. I have to trust you and you have to trust me. I have to trust you to tell the truth because not telling the truth can lead to trouble. Sooner or later, the truth will emerge, the truth will come out as the questioning goes on."

Now a look of guilt, and Trent was certain that the boy had had a moment of planned deception and then had discarded the idea. An errant thought, probably, that had nothing to do with the interrogation, or a possibility that had blossomed for a moment. There often came a time in an interrogation when the subject wavered, drifted away. Or sometimes contemplated a new approach. Or even decided to lie. Body movements often tipped Trent off to that kind of thing. But the flash had come and gone so quickly in the boy's mind that only a slight body movement had occurred. Now the boy sagged a bit in the chair, indicating that a crisis had been reached and passed.

"Did you see anyone else?" Trent asked, allowing the moment to pass but on the alert now. He had been on the alert from the beginning, of course, but now he had an acute focus for his alertness, the possibility of deception.

The boy seemed to go blank, eyes dulled, body slumped.

"Let's take a break," Trent said.

Although it was risky, Trent sometimes paused in an interrogation, depending on the situation. His instincts told him that this was the proper moment to leave the boy suspended, allow him a moment or two of reflection. Other times, it was important to build inexorably, without interruption, toward the climax, confession and revelation. But that would come later.

The boy frowned, surprised at the suggestion.

"I think a break would do some good," Trent said. "I'll step out for a moment or two. Would you like something to drink? I can bring you back a soda."

Trent, of course, would not bring back a drink, would pretend he had forgotten. But planting the idea of a refreshment would make the boy aware of his thirst.

"Thanks," Jason said, glad of the break but still uneasy. The questioning had not gone as he'd expected and he wasn't sure about where things stood at the moment. Was he doing okay? He felt like he was back in school, not knowing whether he had passed or failed a test or picked the right answer in a multiple-choice quiz.

Trent almost ran into Sarah Downes when he stepped into the hallway. She was standing immediately outside the door. Braxton and the senator were not in sight.

He was pleased to see her, a sudden and unexpected flash of brightness in the bleakness of headquarters.

"Keeping watch?" he asked, a bit of teasing in his voice.

"I'm interested," she said. "And I always pace the floor when I'm killing time." Sighing, she said: "How's it going?"

He shrugged. "We're only in the preliminary

stage. He seems like a nice kid. Well-mannered, apparently sincere." For her sake, he didn't emphasize *apparently*.

She gave him a wisp of a smile. "That's nice to hear."

"Any new developments?"

"I think they've stopped looking for new developments, although Braxton keeps sniffing around. He never sleeps, literally."

Trent didn't take her up on Braxton's sleeping habits.

"Otherwise, nothing's going on," she said. "They figure you've got the proper suspect, the perp, in there. Unless . . ."

"Unless I find him innocent."

"Do you think you will?"

Was there a challenge in her voice?

Why did this young woman disturb him? Why was it important to justify himself to her?

"If he's innocent, I'm going to find out," he replied, aware again of her cologne, feminine and subtle.

"I hope so," she said, reaching out and, surprisingly, touching his arm. "I'm sorry if I seemed so negative, so abrasive, in the car. I realize how hard your job can be. I apologize."

"No apology necessary," Trent said.

He felt suddenly cheered, as if someone had opened a window, allowing a fresh breeze to invade the hallway.

"I'd better get back," he said, although reluctant to end the conversation. "I wanted the boy to have a few minutes alone. The line of questioning so far has thrown him off balance a bit. I think the stage is set for the next level."

He wondered why he was telling her this, why it seemed important that she should know what he was doing.

"Good luck to both of you," she said.

Trent was pleased that her voice didn't convey the sarcasm he had expected.

Jason was thirsty, his throat parched, his mouth so dry that his tongue seemed to have swelled up. Funny, but he hadn't realized he was thirsty until Mr. Trent said he'd bring him back something to drink. He noticed for the first time the absence of windows in the room.

Mr. Trent puzzled him. He seemed friendly, like he really wanted to help find out who had murdered Alicia, wanted to help Jason remember what had really happened that day, but at the same time there was something about his questions. Jason used the word *strange* for want of a better word. He couldn't figure Trent out or what he wanted Jason to say. Sometimes he seemed unfriendly, like Jason had done something wrong, had broken a rule, a rule Jason didn't even know about. And those eyes of his. Like black marbles but alive, that didn't blink very much, that seemed to look right into your brain.

On top of all that, he felt that Mr. Trent was disappointed with his responses. Maybe right now, this minute, he was reporting to that detective that the questioning wasn't going very well. A dawn of hope: Maybe they'd decide to call the questioning off and he'd be free to go home.

Jason wondered whether the other guys had done well, had answered all the questions correctly, had even remembered something that would be vital, provided clues that might lead to solving the murder, catching whoever had killed poor little Alicia.

He also wondered whether he should tell Mr. Trent what he hadn't told the detective about that afternoon, but he discarded the thought. Mr. Trent's job was to find out about suspicious strangers in town. Or people out of context. Anyway, Jason wasn't sure about what exactly *had* been going on between Alicia and Brad. If anything had been going on after all.

Sadness welled up within him as he thought of Alicia and the last time he had seen her, not knowing it would be the last time. How he wished he had seen something to help the investigation. How he wished Mr. Trent would help him remember a suspicious person he might have forgotten about, although Jason didn't think that was likely. How could he forget something that important so completely? Yet the police, and especially Mr. Trent, who was supposed to be an expert at stuff like that, certainly knew more than he did about how the memory worked. In fact, Jason was kind of awed by the way the questioner seemed to know sometimes what he was thinking, like when he had that wild idea about making up a suspicious person.

Better be careful, Jason, he warned himself.

Why should I be careful?

A nagging thought just below the surface of his mind gave him an uneasy feeling again, the feeling that something was wrong, that things were not what they seemed. Was that his imagination or just being in this small office, no air-conditioning, not even an electric fan? For some reason, the blank walls bothered him. No pictures. And no windows.

I want to get out of here.

He realized that he *could* get out of there. He could simply get up and leave. He didn't have to even speak to anybody. Hadn't they said this was voluntary? He was a volunteer. Well, he didn't feel like being a volunteer anymore. He wanted to go home.

Jason pushed back his chair, winced at the scraping sound on the bare wooden floor and made his way to the door.

The office was empty, the boy gone.

Trent stepped back into the hallway, saw Sarah Downes disappearing around the corner at the far end and no one else in sight. The boy had obviously left the building, most likely escaping through the rear entrance. The word *escape* gave Trent a measure of satisfaction. Escape was certainly an indication of guilt. Why would the boy flee if he was innocent?

Hurrying down the hallway to the rear door, he swung it open and stepped, blinking, into a blast of sunlight.

Waiting for his eyes to adjust, Trent saw the outlines of two cruisers parked at haphazard angles and a figure approaching an overflowing Dumpster. As his vision cleared, he saw that the figure was a derelict about to forage in the Dumpster.

He spotted the boy standing at the entrance of the parking area, shoulders drooping, head down as if studying the pavement for answers to questions that Trent could only guess at.

"Jason," he called.

The boy glanced up, saw Trent, frowned, swayed slightly as if trying to make up his mind whether to stay or leave.

"Stay, please," Trent said, going toward him.

Why was he keeping the kid here? If he left, alarms would sound and a search would be launched and all of it would point to the boy's guilt.

I need him. I need him to confess to me.

"I'm sorry," the boy said.

They stepped into the shadows of an ancient brick building, its walls scrawled with graffiti. Trent checked the cruisers, saw that they were unoccupied. The derelict was busy looking through the debris on top of the Dumpster.

"What made you leave?" Trent asked, genuinely curious.

"I want to go home. I don't have anything to tell you."

"Let me be the judge of that. But you can't leave like this. It makes you look suspicious."

Startled, the boy could only repeat the word. "Suspicious?"

"Look, no one has seen you leave. Let's go back inside. You may have more information than you think you have."

A cruiser swerved into the lot and pulled up in front of them, the sunlight flashing on the windshield. They stepped aside to let it pass.

"Okay," said the boy, sighing, doubt still in his eyes. He seemed frail, vulnerable. "Okay," he said again.

And allowed Trent to lead him back inside police headquarters.

"Let's forget that you tried to escape, all right?" Trent knew it was important to enter that vital word into the record and he leaned back with satisfaction, waiting for the boy's answer.

"All right," Jason said, glad to change the subject and move on with the questioning and get it over with. Yet he was dimly bothered by that word *escape*. Like he'd had a reason to run away besides just wanting to get out of there. Like he was guilty of something.

"Before we go back to what you witnessed on Monday, let me ask you some questions about Alicia. You were friends, weren't you?"

Jason nodded, relieved to be off on another subject, even if it was a sad subject.

"Let's see. You're twelve and she was seven, and yet you were friends. Did that seem unusual to you?"

"She was a nice little kid. And she was always happy to see me." Which was more than he could say about Brad and some other kids in the neighborhood, he thought, but didn't bother Mr. Trent with that information.

"You liked visiting her?"

"Sure." He wouldn't have visited her if he hadn't liked her.

"You said earlier that you helped her with the jigsaw puzzle. What was the subject of the puzzle?"

"A cardinal. The bird. Big. It practically covered the whole card table she'd set up on the patio. A thousand pieces. She was very good at spotting pieces. And it was a hard puzzle because all the red colors looked alike, just shaded a little. I could hardly tell them apart but she didn't make . . ." And he stopped.

"Didn't make what?"

Jason realized how quickly Mr. Trent picked up on anything he didn't want to talk about.

Mr. Trent waited patiently.

What was the harm in telling him? "Make fun of me," he said. Knowing how pathetic he sounded.

"Like the other kids, you mean?"

Jason nodded. Each admission he made depressed him. He had a feeling that he was telling this man too much about himself.

"Did Alicia make fun of you sometimes, though? You know, good friends sometimes poke fun at each other. Did Alicia?"

Jason smiled at a sudden memory. Alicia mocking him when he finally did manage to place a piece in the puzzle, imitating the careful way he would fit the piece into the slot, humming as he did so, a habit he had developed whenever he accomplished something. She imitated him perfectly.

"Yes," Jason said, his voice gentle with reminiscence and sadness, too, acknowledging again that she was dead.

"Did this upset you?"

"No." But the image of Alicia dead and the way she must have looked hidden under the brush and branches when they found her caused him to shudder a bit.

"You seem upset at the memory of Alicia poking fun at you," Trent said.

"No . . . I mean, it's not that," Jason said, discombobulated now, confused by the sad memory and Mr. Trent's sudden question. "I was thinking of her just now. How it must have been, you know, how she must have looked when they found her in the woods."

"How did she look?"

"Terrible, all covered over like that."

"Covered over with what?"

"Branches and bushes and stuff."

"Does that upset you?"

The question, in fact this entire line of questioning, made Jason pause before replying. He didn't want to talk anymore about these things with a stranger like this man. It was like Trent was trying to peek into his heart.

"I don't want to talk about it," Jason said.

"About Alicia and the way she was found?"

Jason nodded.

"I realize how tough this must be for you, since she was such a good friend. But sometimes it's better to talk. Instead of keeping it all inside. Maybe this questioning can help you personally as well as help the investigation."

"How can it help me?" Jason asked, mollified a bit. Mr. Trent's voice had become soft and tender, his attitude suddenly sympathetic.

"There are such things as trauma, Jason. Shock. When something like this happens, the death of a friend, it can affect you emotionally, deeper than you think. And it's sometimes good to express your sadness and your anger and your regret . . ."

"Regret?" The word sounded strange.

"Something you're sorry about."

"I'm sorry Alicia's . . . I mean, I'm sorry about what happened to Alicia, but what else can I be sorry about?"

"That's for you to say, Jason. That's a question you have to answer. I can't answer for you."

Jason, puzzled and confused again, was aware of his thirst returning. Mr. Trent had forgotten to bring him a drink. His mouth was dry, tongue parched. He was afraid he might choke if he tried to swallow. He had heard somewhere that swallowing was a reflex action, that people couldn't help swallowing. Suppose he swallowed now and began to choke? He was aware, too, that he was sweating, that his T-shirt was stuck to his back, the perspiration like glue between his flesh and the cloth. He gulped in sudden panic. When he spoke, his voice emerged in a kind of croak, like a frog's voice.

"What?" Mr. Trent asked.

Jason was relieved that he had found enough spit to swallow without choking. "I'm thirsty," he said. "Can I have a glass of water?"

He saw the questioner hesitate.

"I won't try to escape again," he said, immediately sorry that he had used the word.

"You seem upset. Upset about being sorry?"

"I'm just thirsty," Jason said.

"All right," Trent said. "I'll find you something to drink. You're important to this investigation, Jason, and if having a drink will make you feel better, then you'll have your drink."

Why did the words sound threatening? Like his thirst was some kind of admission. But of what?

Trent went to the door, knowing that he was departing from protocol, breaking the rules. But his success was largely the result of following his instincts and his instincts here told him to tread lightly, to treat the boy gently, to gain his entire confidence. He wondered if Sarah was back in the corridor with any news.

The corridor was empty.

He looked for a vending machine, found one tucked in an alcove near the back entrance.

Returning with a can of Coke Classic cold in his hand, he waited for a moment outside the door, hoping for a glimpse of someone, anyone. Suddenly lonely, an emotion foreign to him, he went into the office.

Jason received the Coke with a murmur of thanks and asked: "Did you get one, too?"

Trent shook his head. He suspended all hunger and thirst during interrogations, but the question surprised him. Subjects never considered him beyond his role as an interrogator, never made any personal remarks or inquiries. This sudden recognition of himself as a person by this boy made him pause. He watched the boy gulping the Coke greedily, his Adam's apple bobbing, his hand trembling slightly. Trent knew a moment of misgiving. This boy, vulnerable, defenseless, with no knowledge of what awaited him.

Time to get out, Trent thought. Get this over with and collect his due from the senator. And somehow make his own escape.

"Shall we begin again?"

The boy, obviously refreshed, the caffeine probably percolating through his veins, nodded, eagerness bright in his eyes. "Okay," he said.

Trent regretted the loss of intensity and concentration but was confident that he could easily lead the boy into the heart of the interrogation.

"Earlier, we covered your actions during the first part of the afternoon. Your sightings of the postal carrier and some youngsters. Did you observe anyone else on your way to Alicia Bartlett's house?"

Jason lowered his head in an effort to concentrate, his eyes half closed, trying to envision what Main Street had looked like that hot afternoon.

He recalled a few cars passing by, the sun flashing on store windows, the Walk sign at the intersection of Water and Main Streets, a young girl pushing a baby carriage, but all of it muted, quiet, like watching a movie without sound.

"Nothing," he said. "Nobody in particular. I mean, a few people but nothing outstanding." Then added: "Nobody out of context." Glad to be using one of Mr. Trent's phrases.

"Good," Trent said, indicating his approval. "Then, on to Alicia's house. And now we must be careful, Jason. I want you to be specific about that visit."

Trent watched for the boy's reaction to this sudden switch from his observations in the town to the scene at Alicia Bartlett's house. He saw the boy look away, as if suddenly troubled and doubtful. Have I moved too soon? he wondered.

Jason was regarding the blank wall, as if he could find the answer to his question there. The question: Was this the moment to tell what he hadn't told the detective? About Brad and Alicia and how they seemed mad at each other on Monday, not only about the puzzle but about something else.

"Brad, her brother, was there on Monday swimming with his friends in the pool," Jason began.

Mr. Trent looked at him quizzically. But didn't say anything.

"They seemed to be fighting," Jason said. "I mean, not really fighting but mad at each other."

Mr. Trent was still silent, which encouraged Jason to go on.

"I had a feeling something was wrong between them, that maybe Brad had done something to her."

Trent listened patiently, waiting for the boy to make his point but realizing that he was struggling to express himself. Trent's attention was drawn to the boy's hands, active, fluttering, moving away from his body as if trying to express what he was attempting to say. Trent leaned forward a bit, knowing by the movement of his hands, his entire body, that the boy was revealing the truth, whatever the truth might be.

"Brad was always teasing her," the boy said. "He teased everybody. But he was, like, more than teasing her on Monday."

The boy's eyes half-closed again, an indication that he was fully concentrating, trying to pin down a memory or bringing vital information to the surface of his mind.

"She said to him, 'Haven't you done enough today?' Something like that."

The boy sighed, a huge sigh, and blew air out of his mouth as if he had just delivered a monumental message.

"Why didn't you tell the detective about this?" Trent asked.

"I don't know. I didn't think it was important. Alicia and Brad were always . . ." The boy shrugged, losing his struggle to find the proper words.

"Bickering?" Trent supplied. "Arguing?"

Jason nodded. "That's right."

"Why did you think the exchange between them that day was so different?" Trent asked.

"It wasn't, I guess," the boy said. "That's why I didn't mention it to the detective." Then, looking directly at Trent, an appeal in his eyes: "Do you think it was important? Did I do something wrong?"

Trent tried not to show his surprise at the boy's

remarks. Astonishingly, the boy seemed to be suggesting that the girl's brother was somehow implicated in the girl's murder. That they quarreled on the day she was killed, which could provide a motive. Trent recalled that the brother had an alibi, although he knew that alibis could be manufactured. Was it worth looking into? *Should* it be looked into? If it was, the present situation could be disrupted. And it mustn't be. *Jason Dorrant is my subject, not the girl's brother.*

"What do you think, Mr. Trent?" Waiting for a reply.

"I think you did the right thing, Jason, by not saying anything," Trent said. *I can't let this thing get away from me.* "The kind of information you're talking about is too vague and can only confuse an already complicated case. The police made a thorough investigation of everyone involved in the case, including members of the family. I understand Alicia's brother accounted for his movements that afternoon. He spent the entire time with his friends."

"Okay," the boy said, accepting Trent's judgment, settling back in the chair as if relieved that a decision about something that had been bothering him had been made to his satisfaction.

Trent paused, wondering if this was the moment for the preliminaries to be over, when he should launch the strategy that would lead to the inevitable climax. Noting the gathering heat in the room, the moistness of the boy's flesh, particularly the beads of perspiration on his forehead, Trent decided to go ahead. Take the risk.

"Tell me, Jason, about Alicia Bartlett and how you felt about her."

Amazingly enough, the boy didn't seem upset or perturbed by the sudden change of topic.

"She was a nice little girl and I liked hanging out with her sometimes. She was smart as anything but she was what my mother calls a fusser. I mean, she was great at making those jigsaw puzzles but she'd moan and groan trying to pick the right pieces and then she'd place five or six in a row and look at me with a big smile on her face."

"A bright little girl," Trent said.

"She was way smarter than me," the boy said. "One day she tried to give me lessons on how to be better at making the puzzles. Showed me how to choose the different pieces, how to start at the borders. She had a good time acting like she was the teacher and I was, like, her student."

"Did you think she was putting you on?" Trent asked.

"Putting me on?"

"Yes. That actually she was somehow making fun of you?"

"Why would she do that?"

"Maybe she liked to tease you, to make herself seem superior. Maybe she was insecure, and had to do things to make her seem more than she was."

"It was just the opposite," Jason said. "She wasn't bragging or anything. She was just showing me how to make the puzzle."

"Or did she want to make you feel inferior?"

"No," Jason said, frowning, thinking again of the lesson. Had Alicia actually been making fun of him? "Why would she do that?" he asked.

"Maybe she wasn't your friend after all. Maybe she only pretended to be."

Perplexed, Jason scrunched up his face. The room was hotter than before, the heat seeming to grow with every second. He squirmed in his chair, felt the sweat gathering in his armpits. Even his feet were sweating inside his socks.

Jason didn't know what to say, could only come back to his original question. "Why would she do that?"

"Who can explain the actions of other people?" Trent said. "Even little girls. Little girls are not always as naive as we think. That old cliché—you can't judge a book by its cover? It's a cliché because it's so true, Jason. It was hard for you to judge Alicia. And it must be hard for you to realize what she was doing . . ."

"But she wasn't doing anything," Jason protested. "She was my friend."

"Was she? You're twelve years old, Jason, and a seven-year-old girl was your friend?"

Jason realized how strange that sounded, how it made him seem like he was some kind of freak.

"Well, maybe not a real friend," he amended. "I really didn't know her that well. I mean, I'd watch her make the jigsaw puzzles when I dropped by her house. Her brother was my friend."

Jason grimaced at the deception. Brad Bartlett

was not his friend but he did drop by Brad's house. How else could he describe Brad? If he wasn't a friend, what was he? Someone he went to school with. Which was what he should have said.

"Didn't you also visit her at school recess sometimes?"

"Yes."

"Then you did more than just drop by her house to visit her brother."

"Yes, I guess so."

"You guess so?"

"No—I mean yes."

Jason was confused again.

"Were you attracted to her?"

Trent had carefully chosen the moment for that question, knowing that it would upset the boy. He also didn't believe it would lead anywhere. Sarah Downes had reported that there had been no evidence of sexual assault or molestation. But Trent had to judge for himself. And the question had to be asked and the answer noted for the record.

The boy drew back, his mouth tightening. "What do you mean?"

"She was a pretty little thing, wasn't she?" Trent asked. Purposely suggestive.

"Kind of."

"Did you ever think of showing her some affection?"

"Like what?"

"Touching her, perhaps. Kissing her."

The boy's eyes widened in surprise, his mouth twisting in revulsion. Hands, feet, body, all spasmodic in protest. Not defensive in any way. Everything asserting his innocence.

Which Trent had to be quick to acknowledge.

"Don't even bother to answer, Jason. I know that you didn't have improper thoughts about her. Pardon me for making such a suggestion."

"I think I'd like to go home now," Jason said, squirming, thrown by all the questions and especially the new ones about Alicia Bartlett.

He half rose from the chair.

"You're free to go whenever you want, Jason. I appreciate all the information you've provided. You don't realize how important you are to the investigation, not only for your observations but for your knowledge of the people involved. And I find your answers fascinating." Each word calculated.

Trent gestured. "There's the door."

The boy hesitated, half out of his chair, glancing at the door and back at Trent. Trent could do nothing to prevent him from leaving but he also knew that as long as the subject felt free to leave he was less inclined to do so. He knew that something else could be happening. There often came a moment during an interrogation when a bond, a strange sort of alliance, came into being between the subject and the interrogator.

"I know how tired you must be getting, Jason," Trent said. "I know it's hot in this office and uncomfortable. But a little girl is dead, she was your friend, and I think we can help the situation by working together on this."

The boy sat back, but on the edge of the chair, clearly undecided about what to do.

"I really need much more from you than what you observed on Monday. You're in a unique position to help."

Placated by the mildness of Mr. Trent's voice and the possibility that he could actually be a real part of the investigation, Jason asked: "How can I help? When that cop came to my house, he said that you only wanted to ask about what I saw on the street Monday. And I didn't see anything."

"Right. But I was told that if you showed that you had more knowledge than that, I had the authority to go further. And as you and I have talked, I've realized how much more you can contribute, how much more you can help."

"But how?"

"By providing inside knowledge, information that I, as an outsider, and even the police, can't possibly know."

"Like what?"

"You're familiar with all the important aspects of the case, Jason. Alicia's house, the neighborhood, the brook, the woods."

The boy sighed as he considered what Trent had said. Finally, he nodded. "Okay." Then tensed himself, hands on his knees, body bent slightly forward. The signs of compliance.

Trent knew that the game of cat and mouse was over.

We now go down to where the ladders start.

"Fine," Trent said. "Now, let's talk about the terrain of the area where Alicia was found."

The boy frowned. "Terrain?"

"The features of the area—woods, bushes, undergrowth," Trent explained. "You're familiar with it?"

"Yes," the boy replied. "We played there a lot. There's a baseball field and some swings and a slide for the young kids."

"Did anyone tell you the exact spot where Alicia was found?"

"Somebody said a few feet off the path, near some trees. They said her . . . they said she was covered with branches and leaves and stuff."

Trent noted that the boy had stumbled a bit and had avoided using the word *body,* which was entirely appropriate. Trent had also done so to make it easier for the boy.

"What do you remember about the area? Was there loose gravel, grass? Was it rocky, overgrown?"

The boy shrugged. "Just . . . ground. Like you find in the woods."

"Stones, rocks?"

"I guess so. I remember tripping on a big rock once when I went into the woods to . . ." Jason stopped, hating to admit that he had stepped into the woods to pee.

"To relieve yourself?" Trent asked helpfully.

"Yeah." Feeling his cheeks warming, wondering if he was blushing, like in school.

"A lot of stones and rocks, right?"

"Yes."

Knowing the boy would supply the answer he sought, Trent asked: "What do you think the weapon was, Jason?"

"I don't know."

Trent waited.

"A rock?" the boy asked.

Hiding what would have been a smirk of triumph, Trent said casually: "Could have been a hammer. If the perpetrator brought a hammer along. If the murder was premeditated."

"Premeditated?" Jason knew the meaning of the word, having heard it a thousand times on television shows, but he couldn't connect it with what happened to Alicia.

"I mean," Trent said, "if someone had planned Alicia's murder in advance. But I don't think it happened that way. Do you?"

Planning Alicia's murder in advance? Jason shook his head at the possibility.

"No," he said.

"I think it might have been something that happened on the spur of the moment. Not quite an accident but certainly not planned, perhaps as surprising to the perpetrator as it was to Alicia." Avoiding the word *killer* or *murderer,* of course.

"And if it happened that way, spontaneous, not planned, then this brings an entirely new viewpoint to the tragedy."

Jason frowned, unsure of Mr. Trent's meaning. "I don't understand."

"What I mean is this. For instance, if you, Jason, committed a terrible act, for instance, if you had killed Alicia without premeditation, without planning it out in advance but in a moment of panic or losing your temper—then it would make a big difference in the way the case was handled. We would allow for mitigating circumstances. Not first-degree murder. Perhaps your mind was in turmoil at the time. Juries, the police, they understand how those things can happen."

Jason understood. He was aware of different

charges in murder cases mostly from television, first degree and second degree, manslaughter, but had never given them much thought. He frowned as he looked at Mr. Trent. The questioner wore an expression on his face that Jason had not seen before. He looked . . . sly. Jason recalled words from a book he'd read as a little kid. Sly as a fox. And suddenly the import of Mr. Trent's words struck him. *If you had killed Alicia.*

"But I—"

Trent cut him off. That ancient ploy: a question to divert the subject.

"Know what's interesting, Jason?" he asked.

"What?"

"The choice of weapon. You said a rock was used. That's what the police also think. 'A blunt object causing trauma.' Those were the official words. It's interesting that you also said a rock caused the trauma. Why did you say that, Jason?"

"I don't know. There's a lot of rocks there."

"What do you think became of the rock?"

Jason shrugged, wriggled a bit on the chair, conscious again of the heat in the room. He was not really interested in all this stuff about the stone. What did all of this have to do with him? He became aware of a headache starting; a small pulsing pain.

"I don't know what became of the rock. Maybe it got thrown away." He was getting tired of the questioning, despite what Mr. Trent had said about helping out. He wanted, really, to get out of there, to go home.

"I think I'd like to go now," he said. "I'd like to go home."

"Not quite yet, Jason."

"Why not?" Hadn't he answered all the questions?

"Because as I said, you are important. Not only were you close to Alicia, but you spent those last hours of her life with her."

"The killer did, not me," Jason said.

Trent did not reply, merely looked at the boy.

"Then, let's summarize, shall we?" he said.

"Yes," Jason agreed. Summarize. The summary would prove that he was not the last one to see Alicia alive.

"You knew Alicia Bartlett. She was a little girl who seemed to like you. A smart little girl who often beat you at games, made you feel inferior."

Jason opened his mouth to speak. Somehow Mr. Trent had gotten it wrong. But the interrogator held up his hand, like a traffic cop. And Jason sank back in his chair.

"You enjoy reading about violence. Those books you read and movies you mentioned," Trent said, speaking a bit more rapidly, not wanting to give the boy a chance to interrupt. "You said you're not sure sometimes about the difference between reality and fantasy. You daydream a lot. Sometimes about violent things—"

"But—"

Again, the traffic cop's motion.

"You're familiar with the woods where Alicia Bartlett was murdered. You said that a rock was used to kill her. The police had not divulged that information to the general public and yet you said a rock was the murder weapon. Right?"

"Right, but—"

"Opportunity and motive are the most important aspects of a case, Jason. And you had both."

"Motive?"

"Alicia made fun of you. Made you feel inferior."

"I liked Alicia, she never—"

129

"There's a thin line between liking someone, even loving them, and then hating them. A spark can ignite very quickly. Let's face it, Jason. No one else had the opportunity. You were with her that afternoon. Alone with her . . ."

"I was alone with her but—"

"Look, it's understandable. You didn't want to hurt her, did you?"

"No, I—"

"Those things happen. You lose your temper, you get upset, things happen fast, you didn't mean to do it but things got out of hand. There was a rock nearby—"

"It didn't happen like that," Jason said, voice rising in volume, seeming to bounce off the walls.

"How did it happen, then?" Triumph in Trent's voice.

Jason recoiled as if the questioner had slapped him in the face or struck him in the stomach, and his stomach suddenly felt hollow, his bowels loosening. He had a sudden urge to go to the bathroom.

Trent saw the panic in the boy's eyes, the raw pain that distorted his features, the trembling of his lips, his hands raised in protest, his body suddenly shriveling as if he needed to make himself smaller, to squirm himself out of the trap he had walked into unaware. And in a blazing moment, Trent knew irrevocably that the boy was innocent, knew in the deepest part of his being, past all doubt and deception, that Jason Dorrant had not murdered Alicia Bartlett. Trent had witnessed too many evasions and heard too many protestations in all his interrogations to have any doubt about it. Jason Dorrant was innocent. The accumulation of body movements, the spontaneous responses, the lack of cunning in his voice and manner, all added up to the inescapable truth. Trent frowned in dismay and disappointment. He thought of Braxton and the senator waiting for the confession, the town outside gripped by fear and suspicion, waiting for him to deliver the goods, deliver the murderer so that they could all sleep easy and not worry tonight if a door wasn't locked or if a son or daughter stayed out late. The senator's promise echoed in his mind. *You can write your own ticket.*

He looked at the boy. So fragile in his innocence and naïveté. So vulnerable. Suggestible. Unguarded, open to being shaped and molded. As others have been shaped and molded—the thought like a moving shadow across his mind. Maybe I'm wrong, he thought. Maybe for once my instincts aren't accurate. Maybe the boy is more clever than he seems. That momentary flash of deception earlier—was that a glimpse into the boy's real nature, into his psyche, where guilt resided?

Trent had dreaded the day he'd meet a subject who would be the epitome of deception, outwitting him in the game of questions and answers, thrust and parry, an idiot savant who would somehow out-guess and outflank him. He remembered the classic description of a perfect crime: so perfect that it was never perceived as a crime. The perfect deceiver, then, would be someone so innocent-looking, so pure and upright in appearance that any possibility of guilt would be instantly dismissed.

This boy sitting before him—was he that perfect deceiver? Maybe, maybe . . . *Or am I only deceiving myself?*

Trent knew that this was the moment of decision, to go on or to stop. Simple, really. Dismiss the boy and send him back to his everyday, ordinary life not knowing the fate he had just missed. Or should he dig deeper? Call upon all his own cunning and experience to find out if evil did lurk in the boy, if his appearance of innocence was just that: an appearance, a façade, a mask.

But you know it isn't.

Trent dismissed the small voice inside him.

"Let's calm down," Trent heard himself saying in his most reasonable voice. "Let's simply look at the facts, the case against you, and then find a way to mitigate it."

The boy shook his head. "Why do we have to do that? Why would the police think that I . . ." He paused, obviously could not bring himself to say that fatal word. ". . . did what they say I did?"

"It's all those things we spoke about earlier, Jason. Motive and opportunity. The absence of other suspects. No one saw Alicia after you left her that day. By your own admission, you saw no one in town who was a stranger or who acted suspiciously. Nobody else did. Alicia's parents, her brother, all can be accounted for." Trent purposely avoided using the word *alibi*. "You can't account for your actions, have no witnesses to what you were doing between four and five o'clock, which was the time of Alicia's death. You have a disposition toward violence. . . ."

"I . . . what?" Astounded at this suggestion. Everything that the questioner was saying was preposterous but especially this disposition toward violence stuff.

"I'm only stating what the police believe. You attacked that boy last year in the cafeteria. Without provocation."

"I don't know about provocation. But he was a bully. Sneaky, too. He did things to kids when he thought nobody was looking. He cornered Rebecca Tolland and touched her . . ."

"Did she report him?"

Jason shook his head, angry at himself for not doing a better job of explaining what had happened.

"You see? No one saw him do those things. All they know is that one day, without any reason, you knocked him down in the cafeteria. In front of your classmates. Everybody saw you do that, nobody saw what you say he did."

Jason was bothered again by Mr. Trent's choice

of words, always leaving a doubt about Jason's behavior. Nobody saw what *you say he did.*

"Plus those horror stories you love to read and the violent movies you love to see."

"I don't love them. I mean, I like them but I like other stuff, too."

"Look, Jason, I am only stating what they think. I am trying to show you the seriousness of your situation. You are their prime suspect. They have evidence against you. No one else fits the profile. . . ."

Silence fell and Trent let it gather. Surreptitiously, he checked the recorder, saw the pulsing light that indicated the interrogation was being taped. All was going the way he had assumed it would go. The boy had stepped almost willingly into the trap, and now the trap was closing around him.

"I want to go home," Jason said.

"Let me tell you something, Jason. You're safe here with me. Once you step out that door, there is nothing, nobody to protect you. Here we can devise a way to help you, keep you safe."

"How?" Eager with hope suddenly.

"By devising a strategy."

The boy frowned, obviously at a loss, at his most vulnerable now, floundering, helpless. Trent had to alter their relationship, must now become the boy's advocate.

"This is the position you're in, Jason. You're the prime suspect."

"Wait a minute," the boy said.

"Yes?"

"I came here because I was supposed to be helping you and the police. But that wasn't true, was it?"

"Not entirely," Trent admitted. "It would have been wonderful to have had your assistance or if you could have provided evidence that would point the finger of guilt elsewhere. That would have made us—me—very happy. But that didn't happen, Jason. And we're left with the only evidence at hand. The evidence that points to you as the killer of Alicia Bartlett."

Before the boy could answer, Trent went on: "I know. I know. You claim that you are innocent. But you see, it's only a claim. With nothing to support it. But let's leave it all aside for a moment and think of what you should do. What strategy should be employed. I'm trying to help you here, Jason."

"How can you help me?" Jason asked, bewildered, finding it hard to believe what he was asking.

"First of all, we can't have any deception involved. We have to be straight and to the point. Keep it simple. . . . Are you Catholic, Jason?"

"We, my mother and father, and my sister, we go to church almost every Sunday."

"Then you know about confession and absolution."

"Yes. But I only went to confession once or twice. I haven't gone for a while."

"So you know how it all works. How first you confess and then are given absolution. You have to admit your sins before you can be forgiven."

Jason nodded, wondering what being a Catholic and going to confession had to do with his situation here, his sudden predicament.

"Well, there is something you have to do before we can take steps to protect you."

A dim warning sounded somewhere in Jason's mind, his body, his spirit—he wasn't sure which or where but was suddenly jolted thoroughly.

Confession. A different word from *confess.* He suddenly saw where this man was going. He wanted

Jason to confess. To confess to killing Alicia Bartlett. Jason almost giggled in his disbelief, a reaction that was as unpremeditated and unexpected as a belch.

"You want me to say I killed Alicia Bartlett?"

Horror, disbelief in his voice.

"If you leave this room right now, this minute, without any admission, there's no telling what's waiting for you outside. Angry people can turn very ugly. It doesn't take much to start a riot. . . ."

"Tell me what happens then if . . ." He could not bring himself to say the word. Would never say the word. Would never do what the word meant he would have to do.

"I will have your voice on record," Trent said, indicating the recorder and the pulsing green light. "I'll go out and run interference for you. Tell the authorities out there the mitigating circumstances. How you're cooperating. Everything will be shown in the best possible light. . . . The atmosphere will be friendly, not hostile. No one will be looking to shut you up in prison for the rest of your life. You'll receive consideration and understanding. Helping hands. It's possible that you can go home today, be with your family. The charge can possibly be reduced. All kinds of good things can happen, in contrast to the worst scenario. Life in prison, away from your family, hated by people in town, your schoolmates. Once you make that admission, we can save you from all that."

"But I can't do that."

"Let me emphasize the situation, Jason. Outside this door, there are officers waiting to charge you with the murder of Alicia Bartlett. Once you step outside, you will have no protection. Your age won't save you. There's a law now that allows a juvenile like yourself to be tried as an adult. Which means life in prison, without parole, or worse. And you'll be looked upon as a murderer. Without any defenses. But there's a way to mitigate that outcome."

"What way?"

"By showing that you are not a cold-blooded murderer, by showing that you did not mean to harm Alicia, that you are sorry that it happened . . ."

"But I didn't kill her."

"I know, I know. Denial is part of the defense mechanism. Because you didn't mean to do it translates in your mind to the belief that you didn't do it. That's entirely understandable, Jason. What you did in one blinding moment gets blotted out in your memory and you convince yourself that you didn't do it."

"But I didn't."

"You see? You're still in denial. And that's the worst thing that you can be at this moment. You must turn away from that denial. And then you'll have a better chance . . ."

"What kind of better chance?"

"A better chance to minimize the case against you. Once you make the admission, then your defense can begin to work. Your side of the case can be presented in the best possible light. People will see your side of the story. They will see that you are really a good kid, deserve the best treatment. I can't reiterate enough how terrible it can be otherwise. The town outside, your friends and neighbors ready to rise against you. But if we show them your sorrow, your remorse, then you can change things around."

Tears were tiny pools in the corners of the boy's eyes.

Trent, for the first time, found it hard to look into the eyes of a subject. He turned his own eyes to the door, as if his glance could cause it to swing open and allow for the entrance of Braxton to announce that the killer had been found, detained and arrested, and that Jason Dorrant was free to go. Which meant that Trent was also free to go, this responsibility lifted—more than that, this act of betrayal unnecessary. Betrayal. The act finally defined.

Turning from the thought, Trent directed his eyes to the boy and his attitude of innocence. But that attitude would not show up on tape. Only his words. He also knew that he would never get this boy to sign a confession, that even his confession on tape would probably not hold up later. But he was not concerned with that now. He had been sent into this office to make this boy confess. Today. That was his mission, and what he intended to do. Make this boy utter the words that Trent must have on tape.

"Listen," he said to the boy.

The boy inclined his head, his eyes beseeching Trent, as if Trent held all the answers and the solution as well as the answers.

"Hear the silence, Jason? Out there in the hallway?"

"Yes." A wisp of a voice.

"It's a terrible kind of silence. It's people waiting

with bated breath to see who leaves this room. A cold-blooded monster who killed a child. Or a nice kid from a good family, who's never been in trouble before, no police record, who's human, makes mistakes like everyone else in the world. People will understand. They will be rooting for you. But you must act first, Jason. It's all up to you."

Trent could see the despair in the boy's eyes, his body drooping with weariness, the trembling of his chin, the tears staining his cheeks. He sensed the imminent moment of success, felt the sweet thrill of triumph, everything else cast aside for the moment, all doubts gone. This was what he was hired to do, what he was born to do.

You are what you do.

Ah, Lottie. Ah, Sarah.

Five minutes later, the boy uttered the words Trent needed to hear.

As the machine whirred, recording the bruised and broken voice.

PART III

Symbolic, Trent thought when he saw the bug—black, swollen, glistening—crawling across his desk. He didn't know what kind of bug it was and watched fascinated as it reached the transcript and lifted itself onto the cover, pausing to rest on the title: *Trent Interview. Subject: Dorrant.*

Trent rolled a magazine into a weapon and prepared to dispatch the bug with one decisive blow. But it began to move again and Trent swept it off the desk with the magazine, watching it spin through the air, land upright and scurry away to a far corner of the office.

He turned his attention to the transcript with its

pebbled black cover, finding it irresistible as usual. *Trent Interview. Subject: Dorrant.* He reached for it, opened it, thinking: one more time, the transcript impossible to ignore, like a scab to which your finger keeps returning.

He stared at the words on the page but derived no meaning from them, as if they were hieroglyphics, impossible to decipher.

Inevitably, he thought of the small office in Monument and the boy and, of course, Sarah Downes. And most of all he thought, against his will, of that scene in the hallway at police headquarters in Monument, moments after he had walked out of the small office, leaving behind the boy sitting stunned and silent in the chair, disbelief in his eyes.

Looking down the corridor, Trent had seen Sarah Downes emerging from an office at the far end. She spotted him at once, an eager smile appearing on her face. He closed the door behind him, leaving the boy alone to contemplate what he had done. He smiled at Sarah as she hurried toward him. He realized how beautiful she became when she abandoned her cool elegance.

Trent waited, audiocassette in hand, savoring

the sweet moment. Her heels clicked on the warped old wooden floor. As she approached, she glanced at the cassette, her eyes lingering on it. Trent wondered if the office had been bugged, if she already knew about the boy's confession, the boy's voice captured forever on tape.

When she came to an abrupt stop before him, her lilac scent was diluted by a hint of perspiration, which somehow made her seem dearer. She frowned, her jaw tightening as she again looked at the cassette.

"Is that what I think it is?" she asked.

"Yes," Trent said. "The boy confessed. It's here on tape." Suppressing his excitement. Surprising himself by the excitement he felt.

He offered her the cassette, as if it were a gift.

"That's not possible," she said, shaking her head.

"But it is."

"You made him confess." Not a question but a statement. Voice flat. More than flat, deadly, an accusation.

He didn't answer, knew instantly something was wrong.

"They have the killer in custody," she said. "I was coming to tell you that. The girl's brother. His alibi with his friends broke down. One of them implicated him, then the other. He confessed."

Trent looked down at the cassette in his hand.

At that moment, he heard the office door swing open behind him. Turned and looked, as did Sarah Downes. Saw the boy standing there, wan, abject, eyes haunted, flesh moist and sallow. He looked broken, as if just lifted down from the cross.

The telephone rang, bringing Trent back into the reality of his own office. He picked up the phone, heard the voice of Effie, the dispatcher.

"Still no answer, Trent," she said, a bit impatient. "Want me to keep trying?" Her voice betrayed her unwillingness to do just that. "It's been three days and now her machine doesn't pick up. It's apparently been turned off."

Three days or thirty, Trent knew there would be no response. Sarah Downes would not be calling back. Neither would the senator.

His jaw began to ache, like an old enemy asserting its presence.

"Don't forget your appointment with the chief," Effie said, sudden sympathy in her voice.

She knew what awaited him at the meeting: a demotion not in rank but in everything else. Maybe the graveyard shift, midnight to eight. No more special privileges, no special time off for interrogations. There probably wouldn't be any more calls for interrogations, anyway.

The transcript lay there, waiting for him as he hung up the telephone. Waiting for him to open it again. *Trent Interview. Subject: Dorrant.* Jason Dorrant. Poor kid, but at least he was young, free, not caught and fixed in time, as if frozen in amber. Like so many others. *Like me.*

You are what you do, Lottie had said.

But now I don't do anything.

The nightmares stopped after a week or so and he wasn't sure whether they really had been nightmares or just bad dreams. His father said nightmares were the kind where you dream that you're awake and terrible things happen to you and there is no place to run to. Bad dreams were just that: dreams that were bad.

Jason's dreams were bad but he never could remember them, just the feeling they brought back when he woke up, the feeling that someone or *something* was chasing him and somehow he couldn't run, his legs were frozen or, if not frozen, trying to walk in deep water. But nothing specific. And even that word *specific* scared him.

But what really scared him was another feeling and this one was hard to describe, hard to even tell the doctor about, a feeling that he wasn't really here in the world like other people, not able to connect, like he was out of context with the rest of the world, his house, his family.

Specific and *context:* words that terrified him because they brought back that small office and the man called Trent and what he said Jason did that he didn't do.

But he didn't want to think about that.

Didn't want to think about that?

No, he didn't want to think about that.

But knew he had to think about that.

What he did. No, not what he did but what he *said* he did when he did not do it.

Sometimes the pills helped, but he didn't like to take them because they made a buzzing in his ears and didn't take away that feeling that he wasn't really *here*. Yes, of course he knew he was here, right here in the house or outside on the patio and next week at school but still not here, like nothing was real and he knew it wasn't a dream.

He did not like to be alone. He didn't like it when nobody was around. Like now in the house, his father at work and his mother at the Y and Emma off somewhere. Sure you'll be all right, Jason? his mother had asked, with that worried look on her face, the one expression she wore all the time these days. Sure, fine, he had said, because he didn't want her to worry, didn't want anybody to worry, he was the one who had done the terrible thing and he wanted to carry the guilt of what he did all by himself.

But I didn't do anything.

Yes, I did.

But he could never do what he said he did, what Mr. Trent got him to say.

But how did Mr. Trent get him to say what he did when he didn't do it? Could *never* do it, could never do something like that. Never.

Never?

But if you said you did it, maybe you *could* do it, maybe you could do something terrible like that. Maybe deep inside in that secret place of yours you really knew that you could do it.

But how could I do it?

Not how but why.

Okay, how and why would I do it, then?

Look, you already said you could do it, that you did it to little Alicia, when you could never do anything like that to her. But what about someone you *could* do it to?

Like who?

Like, oh, maybe Bobo Kelton.

Yes, Bobo Kelton.

See, you already said you could do something like that so why not really do it then, show them that you could do it, that what you said in that room was right, really, and not wrong?

Show them all that you weren't wrong after all.

But how could I do a thing like that?

He wished his mother would come back. Or Emma. His father couldn't because he was at work. Hot in the house. But he resisted thinking about the heat. A few days ago, he had opened all the windows in the house, not because it was hot but because he felt like he was suffocating even though some windows were open. He didn't want to run out of the house, didn't want to go out in the street, and instead he had run around throwing open all the windows, even in the attic and down in the cellar, even though some of the cellar windows were all dirty and cobwebby. And it wasn't until later when his mother got home that he realized it was pouring outside and the wind was blowing and all the windows were opened and the rain was coming in.

So he ignored the heat now and wondered about what he should do next. If he was going to show what he could do and really did it this time instead of *saying* he did when he didn't, he remembered that Bobo Kelton hung around the Rec Center a lot, every day, showing off as usual, laughing and sly, as usual.

Jason looked at the clock. Ten minutes before three. Hot afternoon. He knew that Bobo would be at the Center. All he had to do was go there and wait. Across the street.

A beautiful feeling of sweetness came over him. He lifted his head, let the feeling carry him for a while, like a fresh breeze in his heart.

Then he went into the kitchen and took the butcher knife out of the drawer.

About the Author

Robert Cormier's acclaimed novels for young adults have been translated into many languages and have consistently appeared on the Best Books for Young Adults lists of the American Library Association, *The New York Times* and *School Library Journal*. In 1991 he won the Margaret A. Edwards Award, honoring a lifetime contribution to writing for teens, for *The Chocolate War*, *I Am the Cheese* and *After the First Death*. His most recent novel for Delacorte Press was *Frenchtown Summer*, winner of the *Los Angeles Times* Book Prize for Young Adult Fiction.